Kevan A. Gee was born in Rugeley, Staffordshire in 1945 and spent all his life living and working in the small market town. Kevan spent his early career as a farmhand and milkman, latterly he worked at Rugeley power station. It was during his retirement that he discovered his passion for writing. He wrote letters to various local newspapers, expressing his insights on local issues and sharing his thoughts on contemporary topics.

In 2021, Kevan wrote his novel, Eau de Toilette, after gaining inspiration from a local care home where his father resided in later years.

Sadly, Kevan passed away in 2024, at the age of 79. Following his death, his novel has been published by his family posthumously, ensuring that his legacy lives on.

Eau De Toilette

Kevan A. Gee

Copyright © 2025 Kevan A. Gee

All rights reserved.

ISBN: 979-8-3249-0843-0

For our dad - Rest in peace, 'ode son'!

1

The door swung shut behind them. The three, two men and a smartly dressed woman, looked outwards from beneath an expansive canopy. They stood in gloomy silence, seemingly gazing at the manicured lawns, paved courtyard and drive. An observer would have thought they were admiring the shrubs and compact herbage which were set in precisely cut islands in immaculate turf. They had been selected for neatness and reluctance to stray into untidy growth. Shape and form was neat but artificial, almost sterile. No stray leaves or uninvited growth were allowed here, no animals explored and scratched, no insects filled the air, birds seemed absent or muted. This was a landscape easy on the eye but without life and energy, none of this registered with the three figures standing under the canopy, their eyes stared into the distance, thoughts elsewhere.

The older man, in his eighties, thickset, with grey wavy hair, scowled and fiddled in his pockets.

"It's no good looking for cigarettes, Fred, you've got none and you're getting none."

The woman, middle-aged, attractive and smartly dressed glared at her father. Her frustration boiled over.

"This was the last on the list and you've had nothing good to say about any of them. They've all had good ratings and it's not as if money's a problem." She continued her tirade: "bloody hell, Fred, you've got to make your mind up. You complain about your flat, you can't get on with the carers and their companies, I don't know what you want or what to do next. What's wrong with this place?" She turned to her husband Lawrence. "What did you think of it Lol?"

Lawrence, tall and slim, with thick dark hair, knew better than to get caught in the crossfire and merely nodded. He had been married to Mercedes, Fred's daughter, for nearly thirty years.

His father - in - law, Fred Cox was a tough, self - made man. Starting with an old lorry, he had built a successful transport company from scratch. The business had been his life. His wife, Mercedes' mother, had died of cancer twenty years previously, even then, Mercedes had witnessed no show of emotion; Fred was back at the yard the next day. He had never taken holidays and never shown interest in hobbies, work and business were everything: a new truck might spark his interest or a vintage lorry, but otherwise nature, music, the arts were all a waste of time to Fred. With his failing health, he reluctantly allowed Mercedes to take on more responsibilities, culminating in her taking complete control for the last two years. Up to the last six months, Fred regularly turned up at the yard, interfering and criticising to the annoyance of his daughter. Latterly, he withdrew, becoming increasingly truculent and embittered. He had refused to live with his daughter and son-in-law so his apartment with mealtime catering people seemed the best option, but to no avail: his boredom and frustration were a source of continuous worry to Mercedes. Finally and reluctantly, at their wits end, they explored the residential care home option, fulminating in the latest crises. Fred was now at a crossroads in his life. Heavy smoking and an inability to relax had taken their toll coupled with a niggling prostate problem.

Mercedes was tough and capable like her father and with Lawrence, managing accounts and logistics, they were a good team. Fred was generally disparaging of Lawrence. He started with the company as an office boy and advanced steadily. He worked hard. When they became an item, Mercedes fought his corner against her father's animosity. Only her doggedness, inherited from her father and Lawrence's good nature kept the blossoming romance intact.

"One of them even had a spa." It was a final plea from his daughter.

"Bloody spa!" Spat Fred angrily.

"He doesn't want to pay." Lawrence spoke quietly, with just a hint of exasperation.

"Bugger 'em!" Fred retorted. "They take your bloody money; they sit you in a bloody chair and fill you full of drugs. And that woman, asking you what problems I had, as if I was bloody invisible! There was a pause and then for good measure. "And it smelt of piss!"

They swept down the drive, past the manicured lawns, past the board with the company's gold- lettered pledge – *Your Health and Wellbeing are our Raison d'Etre. 5 Star rated.*

The Jag, Lawrence at the wheel, Fred in the back, pulled smoothly onto the road. They drove through affluent suburbia in silence. Frustration and weariness muted Mercedes. Her father's situation weighed heavily on her the last couple of years. His bitterness and discontent with his present situation, at times, made her irritable.

"He may as well lie down and give up the ghost," she had remarked. Comments like these would inevitably be followed by guilt and remorse. Even though a difficult man, she was fond of him.

At first, Mercedes thought his flat was ideal, the perfect solution. Not a man to socialise, he could maintain his independence without having to interact with others. She knew he was likely to offend with his bluntness and lack of social graces. Initially, he was continually visiting the yard, interfering. When he finally released his grip on the business, he grew morose, brooding in his flat, upsetting his carers. She and Lol despaired at ever finding an alternative. Was there a solution for an enigma like Fred? Like her father she was practical and tackled problems head on. This problem, however, seemed unsolvable. It had caused sleepless nights. She had begun to despair.

After a couple of miles, passing through less affluent localities, Lawrence pointed to the right.

"Look, there's a place, Mer." She glanced across the road. Fred looked ahead.

2

The weathered, red-bricked wall was topped with eroded sandstone copings, beyond this stood a large house. A board, with cream background and dark green lettering leaned, weary with age. Its nomenclature read - *The Laurels, Residential Care Home. Prop. Mrs R. Richardson.* Either side were two large Victorian houses, one a dentist - *'N.H.S. patients accepted,'* the other was divided between an accountants and an employment agency. Across the road, facing, was a small grove of nineteen seventies, three-bedroomed, detached houses. The large Georgian house stood, as the wall, red – bricked, with worn sandstone porticos and embellishments. The brick wedge lintels, above the original sash windows had, in places, sagged revealed by the crooked mortar joints. The bulky chimney stacks, at each end, leant inward with age, bowing the end walls slightly.

"It looks a bit dilapidated to me." Mercedes spoke with no enthusiasm.

"At least check it out." Lawrence was weary. "What have we got to lose?"

Fred said nothing.

They pulled onto the drive, the car wheels crunching on the earthy gravel. They parked across from the large front door. The paintwork, over the gaping joints was faded, but the brass work gleamed.

After contemplating the facade for a while, Fred's daughter got out and walked to the door. She rang the bell, turned and looked back with a grimace.

Lawrence watched her. She was still attractive, tall and shapely in her heels and white slacks. As the young office lad, he had been ribbed mercilessly by the truckers. They said she had been named Mercedes because she was conceived on the back seat of Fred's Merc. They teased, asking if he had been in the Merc. yet? Had he been in the boot? He was often red-faced and embarrassed, but his good humour carried him through it all. He soon gained the respect of the truckers, more so, because he also suffered the brunt of Fred's wrath. Of course, they wouldn't dare say anything to Fred or Mercedes. They addressed Fred respectfully as 'Fred', but Mercedes, they called 'Boss'. After the ribbing Lawrence received, he always referred to Mercedes informally as Mer. He watched as a tall, cheery girl, tray in hand opened the door. She stood aside to let Mercedes pass through. The door closed.

Fred and Lawrence sat silently in the car. Lol, with a wry smile, watched in the mirror as Fred searched his pockets. He fumbled, irritated, hoping to find an overlooked cigarette. His dry cough revealed the results of his addiction. Lol never bore Fred any animosity and treated him with respect and humour. For his part, Fred rarely spoke Lol's name. "Where is he?" was a typical question, or if pushed, "where's the bloody office youth?" That said Fred rarely used names for anybody, unless decorum dictated otherwise. It was as if he was afraid of becoming personally close to somebody. The only name he used regularly was Merc. Lol's skill, dealing with people, countered Fred's gruffness and smoothed the company's dealings. Fred's business manner was forged in the rough and tumble of post-war survival. Mercedes inherited her father's toughness and tenacity, but was more affable, especially with Lawrence's moderating influence. Business associates and employees however, knew she wasn't to be trifled with.

Although the old house looked weary, it seemed full of life. Lol watched sparrows chirping and scrapping under the eaves. Jackdaws popped in and out of the chimney pots. A squirrel scampered across the lawn. Overhead, in the tree tops a couple of crows 'honked'. Around the house mature shrubs flowered. Rhododendrons, azaleas and camellias grew wide. Some rhododendrons had spread outwards, over many decades, enclosing empty, vaulted interiors. Along the drive, Laurel had grown, unchecked, to almost tree-like proportions. It arched over the drive in a green arbour lending its name to the Georgian gentleman's residence.

Lol pondered on past glories of residences like this, opulent in their day with servants, horse drawn carriages and grand visitors. Their fate now lay with suites of offices, Accountants, Solicitors, Financial advisors. Dentists and private healthcare practices were often found in these aging edifices. The high ceilings lent an air of exclusivity to their clients. The conversion of many of these grand houses to residential and nursing homes suited their voluminous interiors. To most small scale, one owner businesses, the cost of restoration was beyond their finances, hence the tired and faded aspect they often portrayed.

In the back of the Jag, Fred was oblivious to the building, grandiose or ramshackle. He didn't notice or care for the fauna. As for the raucous calls of the crows, it was just a bloody noise. The only nature he took notice of was the weather, would it affect transport schedules? As for animals, badgers and pheasants were a 'bloody nuisance' colliding with his trucks, smearing the paintwork.

He gave up his search for a cigarette and glared at a black and white cat approaching the car, its tail in the air. The cat stared up at him. Fred screwed his face up and bared his teeth. The cat stepped back, looking wary, but its eyes remained fixed and unblinking. At that moment the house door opened and Mercedes emerged. She walked back to the car and leant in the window.

"Well, it's not very posh, but the staff are pleasant and Mrs Richardson seems straightforward enough. I've told her the saga."

"Oh ahrr" Fred's midland accent surfaced. "You've told her I'm an old bastard, I suppose." His accent was more pronounced when he was irritated.

Mercedes put her hand to her head and stared at Lawrence, frustrated and weary. The crunch of gravel drew their notice. Fred watched the plump woman walk purposefully toward the car. She was of medium height. Her unruly auburn hair was grey- streaked with a natural wave. Her face was open and pleasant and her eyes suggested humour. Her mouth had a slight upturn. There was a confident air about her. She approached the rear door of the Jag and opened it, confronting Fred. For a moment Fred was caught off-balance.

"Hello, welcome, I'm Rose Richardson, Mr Cox, or would you prefer Fred?"

"Sir will do," retorted Fred.

"Ok, Sir Fred, welcome to The Laurels. Come on, it's no use rolling up without looking." She reached for his arm. He exited the car slowly, leaning on his aluminium walking stick.

"You're soon after my bloody money."

"Quite right," she laughed. "There's no time to lose."

"How long before I get the bloody sedatives?" The belligerence continued.

"The sooner, the better, I'd say." She winked at Lol and Mercedes. She wasn't cowed by Fred's tone.

Fred, with Mrs Richardson holding his arm, walked slowly towards the front door. Mercedes and Lawrence followed, exchanging surprised glances.

"Don't get excited," whispered Lol, "we'll soon be out."

3

To the left of the front door was a brick and glass veranda. A few residents and their visitors were seated within. A couple raised their hand and were acknowledged by Rose Richardson. Rose keyed in numbers on a keypad and opened the wide front door. It opened into a small foyer with a table and visitors' signing- in book. On the wall, a fire plan and various official documents were displayed. Above the foyer door was a welcome sign. Rose scribbled in the book and still holding Fred's arm, she pushed through the swing door into a spacious hall.

The hall would have been dominated by a large wide staircase, to the rear, but it was now boxed-in with a wood and glass partition and its door secured with a keypad lock for security. Its red patterned runner, secured with brass rods, ran between faded mahogany balustrades. It was topped with a fluted banister rail. It had a spacious feel. Ornate plaster covings, ceiling roses and picture rails, once opulent, now showed their age with wide cracks extending across the ceilings. The paintwork however seemed fresh. The deep skirting boards and architraves were pock- marked with scuffs and dents. Large arched doorways led off the hall, some with double doors. Heavy cast iron radiators were spaced against the walls.

Mercedes noted the worn features, but there was a homely feel to the place. The staff bustled and sounded cheery. There was the sound of laughter and banter from within some rooms.

Rose Richardson stopped in the hall and spoke to the trio.

"Please call me Rose and welcome to our organised chaos. Well, mostly organised," she laughed. "No doubt, you will have looked at our Care Quality Commission reports and found us wanting on a couple of issues. I am always open about it and hide nothing. The team are excellent, but at times, staff sickness or domestic issues arise and leave you with less staff than you would like. If, at that time, an inspection is carried out, an improvement notice will be issued on safety grounds. This happened to us. The other issue has been our record keeping. It has been a little chaotic, partly due to my hands-on approach. I take pride in being involved with the residents. I now have help with the paperwork, so hopefully we will improve on that issue. Well, that's dealt with the black marks, now for our good points. I've already mentioned our good staff. You'll see caring and commitment are good in all reports and our food is pretty good too. We endeavour to provide a good service with compassion and a laugh or two and we do our best. There you have it." She paused, looking at the group, waiting for a response. With no comments, she took Fred's arm with a cheery "come on!" and bustled through double doors into a large lounge.

As they stepped through the doorway, the muted sound of a television was apparent. It was large and stood in one corner, its sound reinforced by sub-titles. It didn't dominate because the room was large and airy. Three large, long sash windows in the opposite wall invited plenty of natural light. Again, the high ceilings gave an airy freedom to the room, an aspect that was missing in the modern sterile homes they had visited. At one end, dark, original oak panelling clad the wall. This was balanced by the light-coloured walls and ceilings. All this, however, was secondary to the people and sounds of conversation within. The house was dominated by its residents.

A few were sat round the television. Against the walls, were a mixed collection of high-seated, easy chairs, typically suited to the aged and the less able; in these sat residents, some slumped, some staring vacantly, one or two were reading. These were normal care home scenarios. Crouched, at the side of the chairs, a couple of staff attempted to stimulate and coax conversation from their charges.

Mercedes and Lawrence, whilst dispirited by the scene, were impressed by the dedicated efforts of the girls. They were patiently trying to kindle a spark from the dying embers of demented minds. It was a job that only certain, compassionate individuals could do. From time to time, the girls coaxed their charges to sip drinks, wiping the dribblings from their mouths.

Fred, not having spoken a word since entering The Laurels now proclaimed gruffly, to no one in particular, "It would be kinder to put some of these down."

"You'll be joining them soon," a voice proclaimed from a group sat at a large, centrally placed table.

"Not bloody likely," Fred grimaced.

The people around the table formed a small group. The majority were men, in contrast to the ratio in the room which was predominately female. The group was a welcome relief from the sights around the room. There was conversation and laughter.

"Come on," said Rose Richardson. "I'll show you our kitchen and dining room." As they turned, a woman in a wheelchair pinched Lawrence's backside, shrieking with laughter. "He's got penguin shoes!" Everybody laughed including Mercedes. Lol smiled ruefully, looking down at his two-tone loafers.

"Don't mind Rita," Rose smiled. "She suffers with a form of dementia which has removed her inhibitions. Her language can be fruity. It was a big shock to her family: they had never heard a swearword pass her lips previously."

They walked back through the hall to another double door opening into the dining room. This had similar proportions and features to the lounge. A television, once again, stood in the corner. Several tables stood spaced in the room. Some had four places set, one eight places and a couple of small two-seat tables. They were set with red paper tablecloths and laid out cutlery. A few easy chairs were placed along one wall. The room faced front as the lounge had done, but a doorway led into the veranda where easy-chairs lined the wall facing the front lawn and drive.

"If you want a bit of quiet reflection or a different television programme, other than in your own room, this is less intrusive than the lounge." Rose, pointed around the room. "When dining is done, you can sit here or in the veranda. These old houses do have the benefits of space and airiness. The downsides are the heating costs. On the other hand, a few draughts keep the air sweet. Toileting accidents are, I'm afraid, a way of life in our establishments, but we manage situations quite well. Come on, onward to the kitchen."

They walked through double doors, across the corridor and into a large kitchen. Stainless steel abounded. There was a smell of baking in the air. Fred wrinkled his nose.

"There were once large scrub-topped tables, but of course, not acceptable these days."

Two middle-aged women in whites with hats smiled at them. "This is Maisie and Betty, our cooks. They do a sterling job. We have a varied menu with choices and these ladies will do their best to manage any dietary requests or fancies. Thank you, ladies."

"I'll show you a typical bedroom." Rose held a swing door open as they entered a narrower corridor. She opened a door into a room with a single bed. It had a couple of easy chairs, a dressing table, a single wardrobe and a small television on a small table. At one end of the room was a toilet and wash basin. There were personal effects on the walls and dressing table. There were photos, some in black and white and a couple of portraits and prints on the wall. The sash window looked out onto a lawn with shrubs. Again, it was light and airy. "We have eight rooms like this on this floor, the others are in a wing down the corridor, similar, but lower ceilings and slightly smaller. On the first floor we have ten nursing beds for bed-ridden residents. A couple of our rooms are double-occupied. Because of reductions in local authority funding, residents who are not self-funded, may have to share a room. It's a sign of the times, I'm afraid."

"Where are the en-suites?" Mercedes had a frown on her face.

"There aren't any full en-suites here, I'm afraid, Just the eight with toilet and wash basin.

Mercedes looked at Lol with raised eyebrows.

"Would you like to see upstairs?" Rose looked at Fred.

"No, that's it." Fred's reply was brusque.

"There are two rooms leading off from the hall. I'll show you one."

The room was similar to the previous one with toilet, wash basin and personal effects. The view from the window was similar, but a cherry tree's leaves brushed the glass. Beyond the lawn were paths, shrubs and, against the distant boundary wall, mature trees.

Rose led them out and across the hall. She invited them to sit in the dining room and left to fetch some paperwork.

"No en-suites." Mercedes frowned at Lol.

Rose returned with her literature and handed them a copy. "I'll give you our details and answer any questions you may have. Of course, the able-bodied can walk the grounds and all can sit out when the weather's fair. We do have regular Bingo and entertainment, usually some keen amateur volunteers. We have got an old piano in the hall which one of our residents used to play.

If you feel you could stay at The Laurels," she paused, looking at Fred," there is no vacancy at present, but one of our elderly residents, Marjorie, is in hospital and sadly, unlikely to return. Hers was the last room I showed you. Please take our literature; if you feel The Laurels could be for you, let me know and I'll contact you at the next vacancy." She paused, looking at Fred and acknowledging Lawrence and Mercedes.

There was silence for a moment then: "I'll take it." The gruff voice was firm and decisive.

Mercedes and Lawrence looked at each other, dumbstruck.

4

Four weeks to the day, the Jaguar, with its three occupants, motored back to The Laurels. It swung into the drive beneath the arching Laurel flushing out small birds across their path. A squirrel scampered to the safety of a large beech tree and disappeared into the canopy.

"I still can't believe it, Lol. After all those posh places we visited."

Lawrence drove with Mercedes at his side.

"I can't believe he's going anywhere. He's only comfortable around trucks, Mer. Anyway, he hates posh and bullshit."

"Either him, or they have got a shock coming, Lol: I'll give it a week."

Fred, who had dozed throughout the journey, opened his eyes as the car drew to a halt.

"I can bloody hear you!"

Mercedes and Fred walked to the door as Lol lifted two large suitcases from the boot. A small company box van had, previously, delivered Fred's few furnishings. Mercedes had tried to make the room homely with a few photographs and prints of company and vintage trucks. What could you do for a man like Fred? No real interests outside the business. No hobbies. No fondness for people and awkward in company.

Fred's father had been a clerk for the Midland Railway. He died suddenly when Fred was twelve. Fred, an older sister and his mother struggled on the small income they received. Fred's sister did the accounts for a small repair garage. The owner, Alf Meddings, also ran two tipper trucks delivering coal miners' allowance coal. Fred got a weekend job helping at the garage. He worked hard and learned fast. Soon he was under trucks changing springs and halfshafts. No health and safety concerns then. At fourteen, he was manoeuvring trucks round the yard.

When Fred left school, he worked for Alf. At eighteen, Fred did his National Service and served, working with Scammel tank transporters. When he completed his service, he returned, working for Alf Meddings for twelve months. Alf allowed Fred to buy one of his old trucks, accepting payment in instalments and some evening maintenance. Fred was on his way. Fred's mother died that year. His sister fell pregnant to a smooth-talking salesman. He soon left, deserting her. She tragically died with complications from a still-born child. Fred was alone, independent but hardened.

His hard work and single mindedness gradually built the company. He married Mavis, daughter of a haulier, when he was twenty-five. She, born to the business, understood Fred's ambition and had a moderating effect on his character. She suffered two miscarriages: they were devastated. After some years, Mercedes was born, a blessing, but not a boy.

From the start Fred treated her like a son. He was fond of her, but hard. She grew up around the business. She had always referred to her father as 'Fred.' When Mavis died, any moderation on Fred's hard nature died with her. Mercedes' saving grace was Lawrence. In many ways, he was the polar opposite to Fred. They were a good match. She had much of her father's character, but Lawrence's influence softened her and gave her the humour, lacking in her father. Now, she stood at the front door of The Laurels with her father, an aging man, embittered with life.

"Well Fred, here we are." She rang the bell. Fred grunted. The black and white cat suddenly appeared brushing round Fred's legs.

"Piss off, cat," spat Fred, with his usual vehemence.

The front door opened and a plump sturdy girl opened the door. "Come in. Is it Mr Cox?"

They entered, the girl writing in the book, Lol following with the cases.

"I'm Mandy. I'll take you down to your room. You can leave your things, then, have a cuppa in the veranda, if you like."

They walked through the hall, past the lounge, where they could see people and activity. A small wide-eyed man approached them. He placed his hand on Fred's arm and gripped strongly. "What date is it?" He demanded.

Fred looked him in the eye. "Twenty fourth."

"They murder you in here, you know."

"Come on George." Mandy took his arm. "You know we don't, not yet anyway," she laughed. George went on his way.

"Don't mind George," she confided. "He's harmless. Just a bit muddled."

"Bloody hell!" Fred didn't hide his disgust.

They could hear the rattle of cutlery and china from the kitchen. Mandy opened the door into Fred's room. It was a fine day and the room was bright. It complimented Mercedes' effort at creating a homely touch. Fred glanced round taking in the lay-out and the detail, noting the truck prints. If he was pleased, he didn't show it. In fact, he said nothing.

"When you're ready," said Mandy, "come to the veranda and I'll bring some tea. Mrs Richardson will be along to see you. You'll be alright here, once you've settled in. We'll look after you."

Fred grunted.

"Well, what do you think of it Fred?" Lol asked: "seems a pleasant room and the staff seem alright."

Fred grunted again.

"Let's go and have some tea." Again, Mercedes raised her eyebrows at Lawrence.

"I'll have a pit stop first." There was nothing wordy about Fred. He had spoken only when necessary.

They left him to his ablutions and walked to the veranda. Fred stood emptying his bladder for some time. His prostate problems created difficulties. Embarrassingly, he also dribbled occasionally after finishing. It worried him. For all his gruffness, he was a fastidious man, neat and tidy. Now alone, he looked round the room, noting everything. His dry cough suddenly erupted into a wracking coughing fit. It left him purple-faced and gasping. He clung to the bed headboard until he recovered. He then made his way slowly to the veranda where Lol and Mercedes were talking to Rose Richardson.

"Hello, Sir Fred. Come and have tea and rest your legs," Rose smiled.

Mercedes found Rose amiable and easy to talk to and had a growing respect for her. As a businesswoman, she had asked Rose how business was. When Fred came into the room, Rose was talking about The Laurels.

"My husband left me for a younger woman ten years ago. It left me struggling with a large mortgage on this place. We manage, just. Ideally, the place needs another dozen beds, but I've no chance of raising the capital. We bumble along. I've a daughter at Uni. doing her finals in social care and a son at college studying music. He sings a bit and plays guitar and would love an opportunity in music. They're good kids considering the traumas they've been through. Still, who knows what the future holds for any of us?

Fred sipped his tea, listening, saying nothing as usual.

"Well, we've got your medication sorted," she addressed Fred. "You'll find things strange to start with, but within a week you'll start to feel part of the place. You must come to me or any of the staff if you've any concerns at all. We have tea at five: it will give you chance to meet some of our residents. All have problems, some more so than others. It can be a bit shocking, initially, when you're new to the place. You soon grow used to peoples' disabilities. There's a lively little group, however and they are a good crowd. I think you'll find them good company."

Mercedes looked across at Lawrence, closing her eyes despairingly. She doubted whether Fred would find anybody good company.

5

At four thirty, Mercedes and Lol took their leave. There had been little conversation. Fred wasn't much for small talk. They sipped tea and chatted to Rose Richardson. When she left, to commence her rounds, they stood to go, Lol wishing Fred the best of luck.

"Ring if you need anything." Mercedes gave Fred a weak smile: she knew any sign of affection would be unwelcome.

Fred acknowledged with a grunt and a slight nod of the head. He watched them from the veranda. They crossed the drive and got into the car. The wheels crunched on the gravel and the car disappeared out of the gate with a toot of the horn. Fred sat staring out of the window, not focusing on anything. A couple arose from their chairs at the end of the veranda and helped an elderly woman out of the door. Fred was alone. The day had left him weary and he suddenly felt very old. He contemplated his fate, ending up in a 'bloody institution'.

Throughout his life, Fred had kept busy. If ever any profound thoughts or emotional issues crept into his mind, they were smothered by business and life's practicalities. Now, with those defences gone, Fred was suddenly vulnerable.

A family of starlings were noisily worm-hunting, on the lawn in the sunshine. Fred looked through them, seeing and hearing nothing. He stared into the distance. He saw nothing: no future, no purpose in life. He fumbled in his pocket for a comforting cigarette, nothing. He slumped in the chair.

A movement at his side broke his trance. He turned and saw a woman standing with a walking aid. Fred noticed immediately that her mouth was turned down slightly at one side. Apart from this affliction, she was a striking woman of mature years. Her hair was short and neat. The sun shone on her auburn locks. Were they natural or dyed? Certainly, no grey was evident. She wore a grey, three-quarter, fitted skirt and a cream blouse. She looked neat and trim.

"Hello: I'm Jane Appleby." She held her hand out to Fred.

Fred rose from his chair awkwardly and proffered his large, weathered hand in a gentle handshake. For all his gruffness, Fred was charmed by this genteel lady.

"I'm Fred Cox." His tone was gruff but gentle.

She smiled, "I spotted you sitting here and know how it feels when you first arrive. It's like starting your first day at school."

She was reassuring and Fred felt comfortable with her. Indeed, his normally impassive countenance softened slightly.

"Would you like to accompany me to the dining room for tea? It can be a bit daunting until it becomes familiar, especially when everyone's gathered in there."

"Thank you. I would." His reply was gruff but polite.

She walked steadily through the veranda door into the dining room, looking back at Fred as she went.

"Let us sit at a small table and you can acclimatise without feeling pressured."

Fred followed and sat opposite at the table. At that moment, Rose Richardson bustled in.

"Oh, thank you Jane. You've taken Fred under your wing. I think I'll leave him in your good care during tea. You can show him the ropes." She smiled and bustled out.

A selection of sandwiches and cakes were wheeled in on a trolley. Jane chose tuna and cucumber, Fred, cheese and pickle. Jane chose tea, Fred – black coffee with two sugars.

"Two sugars?" the trolley girl, frowned: "naughty." She wagged her finger.

Jane smiled: "he needs a boost today, Denise, it's his first day."

"Oh, that's ok then," she laughed, "we can forgive that."

Around them was a hive of activity. Some residents ate and chatted. Others sat silently, breaking pieces off their sandwiches and nibbling. Some looked vacant. The staff bustled between the tables, helping, encouraging, wiping. In some cases, eating was a messy business. Fred was slightly appalled at the sight, but Jane distracted him with her conversation.

She chatted freely; Fred occasionally nodding. Her husband had been a solicitor: he had died ten years ago. They had lived in a large house. When he died, Jane found the upkeep too much for her and she sold up and moved to a bungalow.

"How come you've ended up here?" Fred was curious but blunt, as usual.

"Well, I suffer the occasional bout of epilepsy and at one stage fell, hitting my head. I was unconscious until the postman found me. My daughter lives and works near Brussels. She begged me to leave England and live with her. I couldn't do it though. It would have impacted too much on her life, plus I didn't want to leave and start life in a foreign country. I've been here two years. Last year I suffered a stroke and well, you can see the effects." She grimaced.

"I wondered what had happened." Fred was never the most tactful of men.

She smiled ruefully.

"But why choose this place?" Fred queried.

"A year before I came here, I entered a residential home twenty miles away. It was modern, quite expensive, but had all the mod. cons., it was very comfortable and initially I thought it idyllic. After a couple weeks, I was experiencing doubts. Some of the staff were off-hand; the company seemed to be struggling to recruit good staff, then rumours began, alluding to the mistreatment of some elderly residents with dementia. Finally, the scandal broke and two members of staff were convicted of cruelty: it was awful. The Manager was evasive and off-hand with any queries. It was an unhappy period in my life. An old friend's granddaughter was doing her degree; as part of gaining work experience, she worked here during her summer break. She spoke highly of Rose

Richardson, her work ethic and her staff, albeit with a rundown establishment." She smiled: "so you see I'm here and I don't regret it."

She leant back sipping her tea. "What about you?"

Fred was munching an iced bun. "Not much to say. I had a transport business, but too old and bloody decrepit to run it and too tight to pay for costly care with all the bullshit and blurb."

Jane laughed. She wasn't offended by Fred's colourful language. She sat, studying Fred's impassive features with amusement. She felt she could find a rapport with Fred. She certainly didn't need to develop a false persona with him.

They sat quietly after tea. The day's events caught up with Fred and he struggled to stifle his yawns.

Rose Richardson passed by. "You look weary Fred. Do you want to relax in your room?"

Fred nodded and followed Rose, raising his hand slightly to Jane as he left.

"I'll get the girls to bring you a drink about nine."

At nine when Mandy knocked with the tea, Fred was in bed fast asleep.

6

Fred Cox's eyes opened to flickering patterns on the wall. For a moment he was mesmerised by the movement: he lay watching. The curtains on the sash window were open. Morning sunshine shone through the cherry tree outside. The leaves, moving in the gentle breeze, created a dappled pattern.

The realisation, that he was in a strange place, broke his reverie. He turned away, looking at his watch on the bedside table: it was seven-o-clock. He was surprised: he generally woke about five. He felt rested; he sat up and hung his feet over the side of the bed. Immediately, the cough started. His face reddened and turned purple as he gasped for breath. His shoulders shook. Eventually the coughing fit subsided. He wiped his eyes; the strain had caused tears to flow. He got to his feet and looked out of the window. The morning was bright; his outlook was from the rear of the house. There was lawn and shrubs and mature trees. A fine gravel path led through the shrubbery and beyond. Here and there, in the distance, a rear boundary wall was visible. As he stood, he felt the small, damp patch on his pyjama bottoms: he grimaced. The problem was worsening. For Fred, these leakages had been a severe blow to his dignity. He was tough: pain he could stand, but this.... He hung the pyjama bottoms on the radiator. He shaved, washed and completed his ablutions. He was meticulous in his preparations.

"Christ, bloody pissing myself now!"

His anxiety brought on his cigarette craving. He used to hide some in his flat, out of sight of Mercedes. Lawrence wasn't fooled, he knew his father-in-law puffed a few. Now, however, he was beaten: The Laurels' 'no-smoking' ban was rigorously enforced.

He opened his door and looked across the hall. He could see into the lounge. No residents were there yet, but a young woman was vacuuming. He donned a light jacket and with his walking stick, stepped out. As he crossed the hall, he recognised the plump girl emerging through the door of the enclosed staircase.

"Good morning: where are you off to?" It was Mandy; she was jolly and full of fun.

"Off for a walk to clear my bowels. I'll need it after your food."

She laughed. "If I let you out, you can walk round the garden, but be back for nine, for breakfast. Don't try to escape though or I'll loose the dogs on you." She laughed again.

Fred stepped out: he didn't like walking, but with the nagging desire for a smoke, he couldn't rest. He walked slowly across the front of the house along the drive. He could hear a few cars passing on the road outside. When a lorry passed, he looked up to see if he could recognise the livery. Out there was the real world, a living, thriving world. Here? He grimaced, shutting the thought from his mind.

He came to the end of the house and turned on a path to the side. He emerged into the bright morning sunshine at the rear of the house. He stood for a while, catching his breath. The sun was strong, but the air had that early spring nip to it.

He witnessed a stand-off between a squirrel and a crow. A large chunk of bread lay on the grass. Both were bullies, generally seeing off any competition for food but now they were wary. They edged round the bread on opposite sides, neither confident enough to launch a charge at the other.

Fred watched; he was normally oblivious to nature's happenings.

The crow darted forward and grabbed a piece of bread. For a moment the squirrel was startled. The crow immediately flew up onto the branch of a tree with its prize. The squirrel recovered its composure and ran forward, grabbing the rest: it scampered a few yards, sat on its back legs and nibbled the bread in its front paws.

Fred carried on walking, muttering, "bloody vermin!" He walked along the small twisting path through dense shrubbery towards the rear corner of the grounds. Abruptly, he stopped, sniffing the air. He sniffed again like an animal scenting prey. There it was, unmistakeable, the smell of tobacco smoke. His movements quickened. It was a cigarette and he craved it.

He moved forward then stopped: through the shrubs, in front of the garden wall, was a clearing. Fred could see an old shed, its door open. Sitting on a chair was a black man, smoking. Fred stood a moment then, driven by his need, moved into the open space.

The man heard Fred approaching before he was in sight, but acted nonchalantly. He was lean and long-limbed. He had handsome features with large eyes that reflected humour. He had a generous mouth that seemed to have a permanent smile. There was an air of calmness about him. He looked steadily at Fred.

"Good morning." His voice was deep, but gentle. "Who are you?" he asked directly, but with a smile.

"Fred Cox," Fred replied, not taking his eyes off the cigarette: "who are you? A bloody immigrant, I suppose!"

The man's smile never faltered. "Born and bred here. As English as you." He noted Fred's pre-occupation with the cigarette.

"I bloody doubt that." Fred's scowling features were fixed on the cigarette.

"You'll be half French anyway," the man, teased. "There's not a pure-bred amongst you lot. At least you can tell I'm pure bred." He held out his hand: "Josh Johnson. Have that chair." He pulled another old, tubular, chair from the shed

Fred grunted, shook his hand and sat in the tatty chair.

Josh blew smoke out the corner of his mouth towards Fred, whose tongue was now protruding slightly. It was, as if, he was tasting the air. Josh knew Fred was desirous of a cigarette, he knew he was hooked on the scent. His mouth betrayed a knowing smile.

"What's that you're smoking, Pot?"

Josh let out a deep chuckle, "You don't seem to mind insulting folks, Fred? It's just ordinary tobacco. I roll my own: four a day, that's all. That's my allowance." He blew another puff of smoke in Fred's direction.

"Anyway, why aren't you working?" Fred tried to gain the moral high ground.

"I start half an hour early and have a chill-out before work." Josh's reply was languid, almost teasing.

Fred, gagging for a cigarette, couldn't restrain himself any longer. "Give us a cigarette." He pleaded hoarsely. It was rare for Fred to plead for anything.

"No." Josh was resolute. "You're not to have any."

"Come on!" There was desperation in Fred's voice.

"It's more than my job's worth. If Mrs Richardson found out..." Josh strung him along.

"Bloody hell"! Fred's exasperation showed. "She won't find out. Come on, give me one.

"Well, if you say please," Josh teased, grinning all the time, observing Fred's desperation.

"Come on you bloody foreigner. Please!" Fred was defeated, but belligerent.

"Oh, alright," smiled Josh, "seeing as you're so polite."

He rolled Fred a cigarette. Fred watched impatiently but fascinated with the procedure.

"Bloody hell, come on. Put some tobacco in it, it's all paper."

"That's all you're allowed. Do you want it or not?"

"Give it here." Fred grabbed for it.

At last, the cigarette was in Fred's mouth and as Josh gave him a light, he sucked in his first taste. It was heaven. The verbal sparring with Josh had exhausted him. He leant back in the chair: the tension left him. They sat smoking with an air of quiet contemplation, enhanced by the tranquillity of the morning.

Josh watched Fred out of the corner of his eye, a hint of a smile creasing his features. Fred puffed quietly, comfortable in Josh's company. Anybody knowing Fred would have been shocked. Mercedes and Lawrence would have been flabbergasted, but there it was – Fred at ease, in harmony with a fellow man!

They had sparred, Josh humorously and Fred belligerently. But with only the briefest introduction, aided by Fred's craving, a seed of mutual respect and friendship had been sown.

7

An unfamiliar girl opened the door to Fred. She was slim with prominent cheek bones. She had cropped hair, trendily styled, one side longer than the other. Her hair was fair with green streaks, and she had a nose ring. Fred stared at her, mouth dropping open.

"Enjoyed your walk?" she asked pleasantly, a hint of an accent in her voice.

"Bloody hell, what have you done to yourself?" Fred displayed his usual lack of tact.

"Don't you welcome a little sunshine in your life, Mr Cox?" She cocked her head on one side and smiled. She obviously knew who Fred was.

"Hmm!" Fred grunted. He noticed her name badge 'Katya. "More bloody foreign workers!"

"Yes, but who would bath you and put you to bed if we didn't?" Katya took his arm and walked him into the hall. She leaned across and whispered in Fred's ear: "you haven't been smoking have you, Mr Cox?"

Fred was startled, "no, no, not me."

"Mmm! Maybe I won't say anything," she teased.

She led Fred to the dining room where people were already gathered. A small group were sat at a large table.

"Come on, Mister Cox. You must get acquainted. This is your home now."

Her words shook Fred, the reality of his situation hitting home. He had no wish to socialise, but Katya propelled him to the table, pulled out a vacant chair and announced: "this is Mister Fred Cox, everybody. He's staying with us."

Fred, discomforted, sat down, nodding awkwardly to the group.

"You lot look after him." Katya wagged her finger at the group and bustled off.

For a moment there was silence, then one of the group, a man in his fifties, piped up: "make yourself at home. We are all in it together here, Fred. I'm Spike."

Fred looked across at him. He was small and thin and had a shaved head with a tattoo above one ear. He was sat at the table with a wheelchair behind him. He was perky, with bright eyes and quick actions. He had a trace of a southern accent. Cockney, Fred thought.

"This is Lionel." He pointed to an elderly man, who was sat beside him. "Lionel has been here for ever," he said.

Lionel, although aged, sat upright. He looked tall with a mane of white wispy hair. He had a long face with a large nose and ears.

"Pleased to meet you," Lionel spoke clearly and gently. He had the speech and mannerisms of an educated man, Fred thought. He offered his hand over the table and shook Fred's vigorously.

"Are you here for the long haul?" queried Lionel.

"We'll see." Fred was terse in his non-committal manner.

"You can do worse than here," Spike suggested.

"Yes, the bloody workhouse," grumbled Fred.

There was laughter among the group. Fred's deadpan humour and impassive features brought a new flavour to their daily routine.

"What date is it?" Fred recognised the small wide-eyed man he had encountered on his first visit. It was George: he sat to the right of Fred.

"Twenty fourth." Fred was grumpy but responded

"Oh good." George nodded his head.

At that moment two trolleys were wheeled in: coffee and tea, cereal and biscuits, brown and white bread, butter, jam and marmalade. George greeted their arrival with a virtuosic display of drumming on the table with his cutlery.

"He used to drum in a band," Spike informed a quizzical Fred. "He has to make do with cutlery now."

"May I sit here?" a voice said at Fred's side. It was Jane Appleby. She sat down with a smile to Fred and the others. "We've already met." Jane told the group.

They were just requesting their beverages when a gaunt man of medium height sat down at one end of the table. He had lined, but handsome features, vivid blue eyes and a good head of blonde greying hair.

"Hi everyone." His eyes alighted on Fred.

"Fred, this is Maurice. He used to be a playboy, but now he's just a has-been" ribbed Spike.

"Greetings Fred, how are you?" Maurice flashed his white teeth as he smiled. "Ignore the peasants. They've never savoured the fruits of life. By the way it's pronounced Maureece last syllable as in 'Reece'. A bit of French influence, you know." He smiled again at Fred.

"Bullshitter," Fred thought, but nodded at Maurice.

Fred requested porridge and toast, Jane muesli. Spike ordered bacon and eggs: "you've got to get your money's worth, Fred," he announced gleefully.

"He's not even paying," Maurice announced. "He's a damned free-loader."

"What, we're paying and he's not?" Fred was indignant.

"Too right!" said Spike with relish. "Don't skimp on the bacon!" he shouted in the direction of the kitchen.

Jane laughed.

"Bloody hell!" Fred was disgusted. "We save and bloody skimp. He spends it all and gets a free ride. There's something wrong with this world!"

"I'll have a couple of rounds of toast please, Mavis, to dip in my egg," Spike piped up. He raised his face to the girl and grinned whilst eyeing Fred out of the corner of his eye.

"Bloody hell!" Fred, exasperated, looked round at the others.

"It's terrible." Maurice concurred. Jane and Lionel tittered.

"It's the likes of you that bring the country down," moaned Fred.

"It's people like me that keep the economy going," Spike countered. "We spend our money. You business people would be bust without me. You savers grind the economy to a halt. Anyway, you will have diddled the taxman out of more than I've spent." He grimaced mischievously at Fred.

"What date is it?" George demanded. His intervention interrupted the discussions.

"I told you, the twenty fourth," Fred said tetchily.

"Oh, right," said George.

The group quietened and got on with the business of breakfast. Spike, always active, shouted cheery greetings and comments to residents sat around.

"What are you having for breakfast, Harold?"

"Hmm duck. No not duck. Hmm tags. Hmm bags. Hmm no, no," he said, frustration showing in his face.

"You mean eggs, Harold, eggs," Spike said, helpfully.

"Yes, yes, eggs, yes eggs." A smile broke out on his face: "and toast."

Jane whispered in Fred's ear. "You know, Spike's marvellous with people. He's got so much patience. It's awful for people with dementia, tragic. People have difficulty conversing with them, so they don't bother. Some, like Harold, struggle with speech: some can't communicate at all. Who knows what they think. In the latter stages, I don't think they are aware of their situation anyway. Their nearest and dearest carry the burden: I watch them coming to visit, often distraught, wondering if they're doing enough to help. Guilt weighs heavily on them, particularly when they have to commit their loved ones to care. It's terrible.

Jane was obviously concerned. Fred grunted in his best sympathetic manner. He looked round at the staff struggling to feed and communicate with some of those people.

"What date is it?" George demanded in Fred's ear.

Fred's patience was running out: "Bloody hell, twenty fourth, twenty Fourth!"

"Oh, right," said George.

Just at that moment a rippling, bubbling sound came from an adjacent table.

"I say, that's a bit early today," Maurice looked up from the table.

"It certainly is," Lionel responded: "we've hardly got through breakfast."

"Katya!" shouted Spike. "Duty calls. I think Jack's done his business."

Katya walked from the dining room door. "Come on Jack. Let us get you sorted. Jack accompanied Katya meekly towards the door. As they passed, the aroma assailed them.

"Beans would you think?" Lionel queried.

"Or broccoli," Spike Interjected. "The best incontinence pants in the world won't hold that."

Fred was aghast. He couldn't understand how they could be so blasé. Maurice continued to read the newspaper; even Jane sipped her coffee nonchalantly. Fred was unsettled.

"It's what we call 'eau de toilette' Fred, or as Spike would have it 'odour de toilet', surprisingly you do grow accustomed to it." Maurice explained with a sympathetic nod to Fred.

"What date is it?" George piped up.

That was enough for Fred. "I'm off to stretch my legs." He rose from his chair.

"See you at dinner," said Spike, cheerily. "Need to get your money's worth, Fred."

Fred sat in a chair in the hall and watched the comings and goings. The girls were in and out carrying out their duties. They ferried trolleys, guided frail residents to toilets and bathrooms. They hoisted the frail in and out of their chairs with special lifting gear. They emerged from the lift with wheelchairs. Some of the staff shunned the lift and trotted up the stairs. A trolley emerged from the lift with medications, dressings, ointments and paraphernalia for the sick. Most of the women, girls in Fred's mind, called out to him as they passed. Fred wondered how they could stick the job. He could hear people shouting out and moaning occasionally upstairs. God knows what it was like up there. He found people's afflictions distressing enough downstairs.

He thought of his own, busy existence: work had shut out all the uncomfortable realities of life. In truth, Fred, tough in business, tough with people, tough on himself, could barely cope with the experience he now faced. He wanted to escape, hide, bury his head: he felt helpless, not in control of his own destiny.

He stood abruptly and shuffled across to his room, on the far side of the hall. The pressure on his bladder was unbearable. In his room, he unzipped at the toilet, only just in time, peeing on the floor in his haste.

"Dear God!" he thought. "What the bloody hell's happening to me?" He noticed his pyjama bottoms had been removed from the radiator. They knew. He bent and mopped the floor with some toilet paper: the bending and stress instigated a coughing fit. The wracking cough coloured his face as he gasped for breath. He struggled to the bed and flopped down. He lay looking at the ceiling. For the first time, that he could recall, he felt afraid.

8

A knock on the door aroused Fred.

"Can I come in?" a cheery voice asked. Hearing no answer, Rose Richardson opened the door and peered round the opening. "Hello, Fred. You didn't come for elevenses, Jane told me. Are you ok?" She walked slowly into the room. "May I sit here?" She smiled, pointing to an easy chair.

Fred sat up quickly, embarrassed to be found reclining.

"Stay where you are." Rose held her hand out.

The exertion started Fred's cough. When it ceased, he lay back on the pillow.

Rose, not only a compassionate woman, but also a shrewd judge of character, scrutinised Fred with a keen eye. Over the years, she had watched residents come and go; most lived out their days happily here: she could only recall a couple of people who had left after a few days, unable to cope. She had witnessed people with advanced dementia who had been sectioned or committed to the home; it was always distressing. She had welcomed people with terminal illnesses to nursing care on the first floor. Some were upset to be leaving their homes. Some were oblivious. There was a common misconception that all dementia patients were sedated: this was not so here. Rose and her staff did their best to keep her charges as active as possible. They were integrated with the other residents, if possible. Only if they became a danger to themselves and others, was sedation considered. As their disabilities increased and mental capacities declined, then inevitably they slumped in their chairs. This was typical of the unfortunates in the latter stages. In those circumstances, keeping them comfortable, with dignity, was the best that could be achieved.

Fred, Rose knew, belonged to that section of society who had been fully independent, self-motivated and immersed in their work. She knew that coming to The Laurels wasn't the biggest issue for people like Fred, but the loss of a place in society, the loss of purpose in their lives. In short, they felt they were thrown on life's scrapheap. Life was over. They had known nothing else but their work.

"We will need to keep our eye on that cough, Fred. "She was leading in to the more sensitive topic. "And how are you finding it, Fred? Tricky, I suppose," she answered herself, shielding Fred from what she knew would be difficult conversation for him.

"It's tough going, Fred, I know, this first week. It's a completely new life, alien to what you've experienced. You must give it a chance. It will be difficult for a man like you, but if you can stick it out for this week, you will find things easing. You may not be a sociable person in the manner of Spike or Lionel, but trust me you'll find a niche. Give it a go."

She smiled at Fred, patting his hand. Fred's impassive face showed no discernible reaction. His heavy jowls, set jaw and permanent scowl rarely changed. Only people who knew him well, or observant, attuned individuals, like Rose, could detect the subtle changes in his demeanour. Those that knew him had probably never seen Fred laugh and a smile would constitute only a slight movement of his mouth and eyes. He was an undemonstrative man, uneasy with emotion. Any outward display in others, though tolerated, was a sign of weakness to Fred. 'Grit your teeth and get on with it' was Fred's tenet.

"Listen Fred, if that prostate problem becomes a worry, me come and talk to me. We can tackle anything here. There should be no embarrassment between you and me. You can speak your mind to me at any time and no doubt you will."

Rose had covered much of Fred's concerns without him saying a word. He respected her for her honesty and straightforward approach. Whether he would persevere, of course, was still in doubt.

"Dinner will be ready in thirty minutes. See you there." Then she was gone.

Fred heaved himself off the bed and peered out of the window. He didn't really want company but made the effort. The midday sun had moved to the side of the house, illuminating the garden, but without the glare. Josh appeared, walking along the garden path towards the house, with his long strides. He spotted Fred and acknowledged him with a grin and a 'thumbs up'. Fred raised his hand. What he wouldn't do for a cigarette now. Fred turned away, refreshed his face at the wash basin, combed his hair and walked towards the door. He suddenly paused, thought, then walked back to the dressing table. An incident from breakfast triggered a conscious action; it was his first since arriving.

9

The dining room was a hive of activity: residents were gathering, some moving briskly, others moving slowly with walking aids and frames. Some, although brisk, required guidance to the table, lest they wandered aimlessly. There was a general hubbub; cutlery and crockery clattered. A murmur of conversation pervaded. The louder, stronger voices of the staff dominated, chivvying folks into position, ferrying hot meals from kitchen to trolley to table. One elderly lady appeared with a shoe on one foot and a slipper on the other.

"Hey up, Emily. What are you wearing today?" asked a friendly voice.

A man entered with his coat and hat on. "Is the coach here yet?" he asked plaintively.

"Come on, Joe. It's not Blackpool, today, you know. Let's get you sorted."

Throughout all the pandemonium, the staff coped with efficiency and good humour. Fred was impressed although uneasy with the sights and sounds.

Some residents were pushed in wheelchairs. Fred noticed Spike propelling himself into the dining room unaided. He moved to the large table that he had occupied at breakfast. Fred spotted Jane Appleby sitting with her back to him with an empty seat to her right. Fred had felt comfortable with Jane when he first encountered her and now moved slowly forward to the vacant seat.

"Come on, Fred." Lionel spoke as if he had known Fred for years: "come and join us."

Fred pulled the chair out and nodded to the company. They were sat as previously. Spike and Lionel opposite, Jane to his left, George to the right and Maurice at the left end of the table. It appeared to Fred that everyone coveted their familiar places. Many sipped the orange juice placed on the tables.

A strident voice shouted out. "Where's the bloody dinner?"

"Coming, Rita," one of the girls responded.

"Good old Rita," laughed Spike: "we won't starve while she's around."

"How have you been getting on?" Jane asked quietly.

Fred answered with a "Well...", as if that answered all.

Suddenly, George, who was sitting quietly, came to life. He beat out a vigorous drum roll with a knife and fork on the table, ending with a metallic flourish on the stainless-steel condiment set. The dinner trolley had appeared. The pre-ordered hot meals were handed out. Jane had salmon with a few potatoes and salad. Lionel, Spike and George had shepherd's pie. Maurice was picking at a salad with chicken. Fred had opted for breaded cod, parsley sauce, mash and peas. He was a plain eater: no foreign 'shite' for Fred, none of that pasta 'muck' and definitely no Chinese or curries. There was only one sort of rice in Fred's world and that was rice pudding.

Jane ate carefully and daintily. She was dexterous with cutlery, markedly different to the shovelling motions of Spike and George with their shepherd's pie. Even Lionel was a speedy eater, but with more decorum. Fred noticed Maurice struggling with his food, picking it over and eating tiny morsels. He seemed to have very little appetite. Fred, himself, had a good appetite but was a very steady eater. He had no fancy skills with cutlery, and scoffed at people who ate using the back of a fork. "Pretentious buggers." His slow eating and chewing masked his lack of finesse, not that Fred would ever consider that to be of any consequence.

The speedy eaters were soon finished. Shepherd's pie certainly slips down easily and with dinner devoured George had lost his focus. He turned to Fred.

"What date is it?"

Fred turned his head slightly with the hint of triumph on his face. He reached into his pocket slowly and revealed his master stroke. With all eyes on it, Fred opened a sheet of paper and laid it on the table in front of George, tapping his stubby forefinger on it.

George peered at it: "Oh!"

Fred leant back with a look of satisfaction. On the paper could be read in large print 'The 24th'

George re-iterated: "Oh!"

Spike looked across at Maurice winking, a knowing grin passing between them.

Fred and Jane finished their eating and sat back. Plates were cleared away.

George turned to Fred again. "What date is it? "

Fred again tapped the paper with his finger.

"Oh!"

'Pudding,' as Fred called it, arrived. Fred, George and Spike had treacle sponge and custard. Jane and Lionel had cheesecake. Maurice had coffee only.

"You can't beat a good treacle sponge, eh Fred?" Spike smacked his lips.

Fred nodded.

"It's even better when you're not paying for it, eh? Spike goaded, grinning mischievously at Lionel.

Fred scowled: he didn't know what to make of Spike. "Cocky bastard!" he thought.

"I'm afraid we have to put up with rabble, Fred," Maurice was studying the nails on his long fingers. "The hoi polloi inveigle their selves everywhere."

Fred was distrusting of Maurice and viewed him with a jaundiced eye: "Shallow!"

They finished their puddings and relaxed.

"What date is it? George persisted.

Fred tapped the paper.

"Oh!"

Jane was telling Fred quietly, how Maurice had been seriously ill, when George looked Fred in the eye and asked: "is that today's date?" pointing to the paper on the table.

Fred glared at him. "Yes."

Several minutes passed with Spike and Lionel discussing the economy. George leant over, looking Fred in the face again.

"Is that today's date?

Exasperation got the better of Fred, "Bloody hell I give up!"

There were peals of laughter from the group. Even George joined in, unaware of the significance, but enjoying it nevertheless.

Lionel congratulated Fred with a sympathetic look. "Full marks for effort, Fred."

"I can't fault you, Fred." Spike clapped his hands together gleefully.

Jane, seeing Fred's frustration, leaned in to him and placed her hand on his arm, smiling sympathetically.

They sat drinking their coffees and tea for some time. Fred was watching staff struggling to feed other residents. Some struggled gamely, feeding themselves, clinging to independence. Food cascaded down their napkins into their laps. Drink dribbled out the corners of their mouths. Sometimes they laboriously chased food round their plates with forks or spoons, only for it to fall off before it reached their mouths. They would then start the slow process again. Fred couldn't bear to look and focused on his companions.

He would have left the table, immediately after eating, if Jane had not been there. He sat it out, for her company. George was quiet now, as if in deep contemplation. Lionel leant back, hands clasped on his chest, eyes closed. Maurice was distracted, looking into the distance fiddling with the buttons on his bright, silk shirt. Spike, perky as ever, was holding a one-sided conversation with an elderly lady in a wheelchair: she had bright eyes fixed on Spike. Fred had noticed one of the girls feeding her earlier. She seemed able to open her mouth slightly and swallow mashed food, but otherwise seemed completely immobile.

"How are you today, Mary?" Spike persisted: "have you been singing again because it's raining outside."

Fred noticed her bright eyes moving slightly as Spike spoke. Her right hand rested on the arm of her wheelchair and her index and middle fingers moved up and down animatedly.

"I think you could talk to me with those fingers." Spike smiled at her. "We'll have to work on it, Mary."

"You know Fred, many people think Spike is brash and loud, but he really is a nice man. He goes out of his way to be nice to people like Mary and he's got endless patience." Jane turned to Fred as she spoke.

"He was paralysed below the waist, following a 'hit and run' years ago. His wife eventually left him because of his severe depression, he ended up here. Since then, he's come to terms with his disability and is a breath of fresh air around the place. Underneath his leg-pulling, he's very considerate. You mustn't judge a book by its cover, Fred." Jane seemed to understand Fred: she could sense, beneath the surly man, a hidden sensitivity. Maybe one day it would emerge.

Fred grunted, noncommittally.

"Shall we sit in the conservatory awhile?" Jane suggested. She understood that Fred was a man who needed pushing, not that he would be pushed by anyone, but she felt she could do it. He was a grouchy man, but solid and dependable, she felt. She thought he was like a big teddy bear under the grumpiness and was at ease in his company. As they walked into the conservatory, the black and white cat rubbed against Fred's legs.

"Scat, cat!" Fred hissed. "The bloody cat knows I hate it. Why does it always come to me?"

Jane laughed. "Well, it certainly likes you, Fred."

They sat in the easy chairs and gazed out the window. A laundry van drove round the side of the house.

"They'll get good business here." Fred nodded meaningfully.

"Well, none of us know how we will end up." Jane gave a sad sigh.

"It's bloody depressing. How long have we got Jane?" He looked directly at her.

It was the most Jane had heard Fred speak and the first time he had used her name, indeed anyone's name. It felt good.

"Well, all I can say, Fred, is we should try and make it as pleasurable as possible and hope we can come to terms with life here. Take Spike: he does a good deed, hands out kind words and must feel a sense of fulfilment. Perhaps we could all follow his example."

Fred grunted. He wouldn't go as far as that.

The afternoon sun broke through the cloud and warmed the conservatory. Fred and Jane drifted into afternoon slumber. They were joined by the cat, who curled at Fred's feet.

10

It was a sunny afternoon. In the conservatory, Fred and Jane watched afternoon visitors come and go. Fred sipped his coffee with a digestive: Jane, tea and a chocolate biscuit. The visitors were a mixed crowd; some, eager to spend time with loved ones, often came daily; others travelled from afar and came when time allowed; many made the effort out of duty feeling some guilt at their reluctance.

"Do you get any visitors?" Fred made an effort at conversation.

"No, not really," answered Jane. "My daughter lives abroad. I've an older sister who lives in Yorkshire and I see her, perhaps once a year. My daughter comes over twice a year and, of course, I'm invited over there, but I won't go now."

They lapsed into silence for a while, pondering their situation.

"What about you, Fred?"

"Well, the daughter's running the business. She can't waste her time on me."

"Does she run the business single- handed?" Jane probed.

"Well, said Fred, she's got her husband. He's the accountant." That was as much Fred could say about his son-in-law. "Mind, she's bloody capable."

They watched cars arrive and leave. In the distance, near the gate, they could see Josh digging in the border.

"Rose told me she couldn't do without Josh," Jane confided, "he can turn his hand to anything, inside or out. Good worker."

Seeing Josh, Fred yearned for a cigarette; his craving nagged.

"I think we'd better freshen up Fred, it will soon be tea."

Time had gone quickly since dinner. They rose, stiff from sitting: Fred groaned, wishing he had his stick. They parted company and Fred shuffled across to his room. He could hear Spike and Maurice plainly above the television in the lounge.

"You talk some rubbish." Spike jibed.

"It's perfectly true." Maurice responded.

Fred entered his room and flopped on the bed. A coughing fit erupted and left him breathless. When it subsided, he closed his eyes and rested. Perhaps he could shut care homes from his thoughts.

He woke from his slumber with a start. The urgency that lately plagued him returned with vigour. His bladder was fit to burst. He stumbled off the bed, panic on his face. He almost didn't make it, but gasping and puffing he emptied his bladder into the toilet. He stood for some time, recovering and waiting for the inevitable dribbling that followed. He considered missing tea, but decided the evening would be long without it. He had no desire for television at present.

Tea followed a similar ritual to other meals. Sandwiches and cake were the teatime fare with the addition of ice cream and jelly. Maisie, one of the cooks emerged from the kitchen with some home baked bread. For most residents tackling 'real bread' was out of the question. Biting and chewing crusty bread with feeble jaw muscles was too much to ask. Then again, some people like Spike and Maurice had lived with the soft sliced bread and had no love for any other.

"Would anyone like some home baked?" asked Maisie.

George put his hand up. "Me, please with plenty of butter." He turned to Fred. "It's lovely with jelly and ice cream." He smacked his lips with relish.

"You've got a big bottom, Maisie." Rita shouted from across the room.

"Well, thank you very much, Rita. I much appreciate that." Maisie assumed a comic frown, looking from one person to the next.

Everybody laughed; even Fred's face lightened. Rita chortled.

"I'll have a couple of rounds of that," said Fred.

"What, Maisie's bottom or the bread?" Spike chirped.

The group laughed, including Maisie. Jane smiled behind her hand, Fred, however glowered at Spike.

"What would you like with your bread?" Maisie asked.

Fred pursed his lips: "butter and jam and don't skimp on the butter.

"Right away sir," Maisie grinned. "I like a man who knows what he wants."

Fred ate it with relish. It was a peaceful tea; George was preoccupied with his jelly and ice cream, occasionally dipping his bread and butter in the ice cream.

After tea, a few residents sat in the veranda, some returned to their rooms. Jane invited Fred to sit in the veranda with her. Fred, with no set routine, tagged along silently. The television was on, a few residents sat round it. Spike was chatting to Mary: she sat in her wheelchair and Spike in his. Her eyes were fixed on Spike, unwavering. Maurice and Lionel were playing cards. Fred could hear Spike instructing Mary.

"You see, Mary, if I ask you if you like fish and I know you don't. You could point your fingers down, like this." Spike demonstrated with his fingers. "And that means no." Then you've answered me, you see and we're having a conversation."

Jane interrupted Fred's observations asking if he'd ever played chess. Fred had not played since he was a kid when his father had taught him. For a moment, his mind drifted back to his childhood and his parents. It seemed far away and fleeting. He had few memories from those days.

Jane set out the pieces and patiently re-introduced Fred to the delights of chess. To Fred, chess was secondary to Jane's companionship. Time passed and they were oblivious to any distraction.

The house was beginning to wind down for the evening. Residents and carers were carrying out preparations for the night. Fred and Jane parted company to prepare themselves. Fred emerged from his room in his dressing gown and shuffled to one of the bathrooms. The shower relaxed him and he emerged refreshed into the corridor. He walked back passing bedrooms. As he passed the last bedrooms before the hall an elderly man staggered out. Fred could see his legs were protruding from the sleeves of his pyjama top. He tottered, clinging to the wall. Fred looked up and down the corridor anxious for someone, anyone, to help. Nobody was in sight. He wanted to keep walking, but conscience prevented him. He grabbed the man. "Come on, let's get you sorted." He guided him back into his room. He sat the man on the bed pulling off the pyjama top from his legs.

"Where's my father?" The old man pleaded.

"He's here." Fred was gruff but gentle.

At that moment, Mandy, the plump carer bustled in.

"Oh, Mr Cox, have you come to the rescue?"

"Got his legs stuck in his top," Fred was relieved to hand over the problem.

"Well done, thank you. If his legs aren't in the sleeves, his head often is."

Fred stepped back into the corridor, crossed the hall and into his room.

Back in the corridor, Spike was looking out from the room he shared with Lionel. He had seen 'old Harold' stagger out and was about to assist when Fred reluctantly did his 'good Samaritan' act.

"Well, Lionel, that was a surprise. I've just seen Fred show a bit of compassion. I might be wrong about him: he may have a heart after all."

11

The morning was cloudy: a light drizzle fell. A vehicle pulled into the drive at speed, scattering gravel, leaving tyre tracks in its wake.

Fred had risen early as usual. His bladder imposed an urgent response. The reality of his predicament and his presence at The Laurels nagged. Cigarettes were on his mind. He washed, shaved and was escorted out the front door by one of the night girls. He stood at the side of the front door savouring the early quiet before the noisy intrusion.

The large pick-up truck was one of those 'Yankee toys,' as Fred would say. It had wide wheels, raised suspension and an outsize blunt bonnet and was red. It skidded to a halt, its bumper overhanging the front step. The driver smirked at Fred.

He was bony-faced, broad shouldered, but lean. He leaned over and pulled his passenger by the neck towards him, forcefully kissing her hard on the lips. She looked uncomfortable. He released her and smirked again at Fred, arrogant and cocky.

The passenger got out: it was Katya.

Fred fixed the driver with a glare. Still smirking, the driver reversed the truck, spinning it round and roared up the drive, gravel raining at Fred's feet.

Katya passed Fred with a smiled greeting. She looked drawn.

Fred couldn't hold back. "Can't you do better than that arsehole?"

"We don't always get what we want, Mr Cox." Katya's voice was muted. She walked into the house.

Fred stood for a while disturbed by the event, then, leaning on his stick, shuffled briskly round the side of the house. He followed the meanderings of the path, head down.

Josh was unlocking the shed. "Hey, you're early."

Fred grunted a greeting and sat on the chair josh pulled from the shed. The dampness didn't deter the duo.

"Well, you've lasted over twenty-four hours. Are you staying?

Fred pondered the question before muttering, "maybe, we'll see."

Josh rolled two thin cigarettes, Fred watching keenly. He leaned toward Josh accepting the proffered light, sucking hard. The effort started a coughing fit.

"Hell Fred, should you be smoking at all?"

"It's too bloody late now." Fred spluttered as the coughing subsided. "Anyway, there's bugger-all tobacco in them."

Josh laughed at Fred's turn of phrase "Beggars can't be choosers Fred."

They sat in quiet contemplation. Fred leaned back, blowing smoke into the air. His tension eased.

After a while Fred spoke, "I don't know if I'll stick it. Christ, it's a depressing place, an old folk's graveyard."

"Fred, you've got to come to terms with it, or die miserable. It's just another stage in life. Do you bite the bullet and stick it out or go back to living on your own? Me, I'd bite the bullet every time."

"It's the last bloody stage." There was bitterness in Fred's reply.

"Well, you either spend the last stage here, in company, or you sit on your own. I know which I'd choose."

A twitter caused Josh to look round. "Oh, it's you. Hello, Robin." Josh reached into the shed, grabbing a tin off the shelf. He opened the lid and withdrew a handful of seed.

The robin was perched on a stake cocking its head, its bright eyes following Josh's movements. He threw seed onto the damp grass. The bird flew down, pecking, watching Fred warily. Now Josh stretched out his hand, seed in his palm. The robin flew up, perched on the out-stretched fingers and took seed from the hand.

"What do you think of that?" Josh was smiling.

Fred was intrigued, but cynical. "Huh! He's like everyone else on this earth, he can be bribed and bought. He'll do anything for food. Give me the tin."

Fred poured seed into his hand and offered it to the robin, which was perched on the stake. The robin stayed put. Fred sprinkled seed on the grass. The robin flew down to the nearest seed and flew straight back to the perch. Fred tried once more, but to no avail. He threw the remaining seed to the floor. "You've overfed that bird." His reply was tetchy.

"You can't buy everybody's trust." Josh was serious: "you've got to win it. You're just not one of us, yet."

Fred puffed his cigarette, thoughtfully. His gaze fixed on the bird. "Bugger the bird. If it wants to pick and choose, it can bloody starve."

Josh shook his head slowly. "Patience, Fred, patience. You've got to be in it for the long haul."

Fred passed no comment. He didn't know if he could stomach that.

12

The week passed slowly: The Laurels' routine unchanging, solid, reliable. This was its essence. It imparted comfort and security on residents and relatives. They were safe in the knowledge that sympathy and care, food and bed, were guaranteed. Within this routine, comedy, drama, tragedy, all played a role.

An ambulance might ferry a frail patient to and from the hospital. A doctor, physiotherapist, podiatrist, or social worker would attempt to alleviate the symptoms of ailing and aged residents. Hairdressers weaved their magic, giving a little dignity to thinning hair and jaded features. Visitors arrived and left. Some were comforted by the contentment they saw; some were distressed by the stranger they faced, a familiar body but alien mind. In the extremes of dementia, a victim of this distressing disease might show complete indifference or even aggression to lifelong partners and family. Local vicars and priests offered spiritual comforts. They offered humour and compassion in equal measure and were generally welcomed, even by non-believers.

The compassion and care lavished by Rose Richardson and her staff eased and comforted troubled minds and frail patients. Death was the only certainty and, for many, a release. In the lounge, a group of residents were discussing such an incident.

"They wheeled somebody away yesterday," Maurice spoke mournfully, "I think it was a lady from upstairs. It's unsettling, I can't get it out of my head."

"It's a one-way ticket here," Lionel chipped in. "Consider the ages of people."

"We're not all ancient, you know, are we, Maurice? Spike protested.

"Perhaps not, but here we are, with a one-way ticket to the terminus. No getting off."

"Hell Lionel!" retorted Maurice: "you're depressing."

Fred was reading the paper but listening to the conversation. Jane was reading a book but turned to Fred. "I'm afraid we have to suffer this gallows humour; although, maybe, it serves a purpose."

Behind the group, Cyril, a dementia sufferer was seated in front of the window. Earlier Spike had been talking to him. Cyril responded with nods and smiles. Spike had a gift for communication and insight. He could coax pleasure and response from a mind closed to the world. Maurice remarked on it, "I don't know how he does it. He can turn gibberish into a conversation."

A family of four, husband and wife in their thirties and two boys ten or twelve, sat in front of Cyril, their backs to him. The woman was large, had a scowling face and looked round disdainfully at everyone in the room. They opened crisps, the boys squeezing the bags till they burst. They ate noisily, like pigs, Fred thought. The woman looked about, challengingly. Fred disliked them immediately but concentrated on his newspaper. They followed up, munching chocolate bars and swigging cola. The debris from crisps and bits of silver paper lay at their feet. The woman was vociferous in a loud way, the others were wordless, other than the sounds of chomping, slurping and burping. The woman, her face in a permanent sneer, addressed, in a loud voice, anyone who might be listening.

"Of course, grandad gets neglected." She paused for effect, pursing her lips and raising her chin. "He doesn't pay, so he doesn't get the best treatment, second best." She turned her head from side to side.

Maurice looked at Lionel, rolling his eyes. Nobody spoke.

"It's alright for those that can pay. They get everything." Her face was a picture of contempt.

Easy-going as he was, this was too much for Spike. He turned to the woman and pointed to Fred and Maurice. "Let me tell you." He spoke quietly but firmly. "These gentlemen pay and I don't, but I get exactly the same treatment and food as they do.

"In fact, he gets more," quipped Maurice.

The woman was thwarted slightly but wasn't done. "Anyway, they should do more for him, get him doing things. They don't do enough." Her voice got louder. "Where are the activities? Why aren't they getting him up?"

Fred couldn't stand it anymore. "What do you expect them to do, get him up doing the bloody Tango? His face was red with anger: "why don't you get off your arses and do something yourself?"

"Yes, piss off!" shouted Rita, from across the room.

The woman was shocked into silence, along with the rest of the room. She glowered at Fred. It was left to Lionel, to smooth things. "There are a couple of wheelchairs by the door. Why don't you get one and give Cyril a spin round the garden: I'm sure he'd love that."

The woman was put on the spot. Her husband rose, quietly. He walked into the hall, returning with a wheelchair. The family rose as one, scraping their chairs across the floor. Rose Richardson was passing by and helped them manoeuvre Cyril into it. Rose accompanied them to the door and let them out. Their heads appeared in the window pushing the chair along the drive. Rose returned with a dustpan and brush.

"Well, that's a turn-up." She looked pleasantly surprised.

The day passed, but today was take-away day: this was an occasional treat. It was anticipated with relish. Upstairs the frail were served the normal menu, downstairs, however, people could opt for the take-away. In fact, the food was ordered and delivered to the door. Fish and chips, the most popular choice along with the usual chip shop varieties. Maurice, Spike and Lionel opted for a curry. Many residents with no medication or health restrictions were allowed a small beer or lager. Rose felt that this small treat boosted the morale and well-being of her charges.

Fred was appalled. He couldn't believe a man of Lionel's age could eat that muck.

"Three years in the army, old man. Three years in India watching the nation torn apart. A curry was such a relief from bully beef."

"I know what I'd have picked," was Fred's disgusted response.

"Where's your sense of adventure? Where's your desire to taste the exotic, Fred? Unwind: smell the flowers. Live a little." Maurice threw open his arms in a dramatic gesture.

"Huh!" One word was all Fred needed.

The food arrived and was greeted with relish. George went into a drumming frenzy, beating a vigorous tattoo on tables, chairs, even tapping on Spike's bald pate, much to the amusement of all.

The earlier demise of the elderly resident was forgotten: life moved on. Why ponder on death when food was on offer? You live for the moment when life is short.

13

Fred woke, panicking: he rushed from his bed, too late! A spreading yellow stain appeared on his pyjama bottoms. He reached the toilet, expelling the remainder of his bladder's contents into the pan.

"Oh Christ, no! What the bloody..!" He was distressed, embarrassed. He mopped the floor with his pyjamas, hiding the evidence. He looked at himself in the mirror: "Christ!" He closed his eyes, leaning on the dressing table. Finally, he gathered himself, put on his dressing gown and opened the door. He peered out, looking up and down. He could hear activity but saw no one. He shuffled hurriedly along the corridor.

He reached the first bathroom, it was empty; he entered, closing and locking the door. The locks were the type that could be disengaged from the outside. The bathroom was fitted out for the disabled, a raised toilet, grab rails, bath with hoist and walk-in shower. Alarm pull cords were strategically hung. As with most of the building, the bathrooms were slightly faded but clean.

Fred stripped and turned on the shower. In his haste, he walked beneath the shower head before it had warmed through. The cold water shocked him and he tensed, folding his arms across his woolly, barrel chest. His head and bull neck were sunk into his raised shoulders. He gritted his teeth and let the cold water purge him. Gradually the water warmed.

As the warm water flowed over him, he contemplated his predicament: what could he do with his pyjamas? Could he find a laundry area to quietly deposit them or dump them in a bin? If he had stayed in his own flat nobody need ever have known. He was bitter.

Fred normally showered swiftly and briskly, but he lingered. The warm water was soothing and soporific, easing his tension, but not his low spirits. He finally emerged, dried off and with dressing gown on, exited the bathroom. He was making his way slowly back to his room when somebody caught up with him. He turned, startled: it was Katya.

"Hello, Mister Cox. Why are you showering so early?" She smiled and took his arm as they walked. Fred looked at her but said nothing.

"I know," she paused. "You can't have a smoke this morning. It's Saturday and Josh is at home." She winked, knowingly.

As they reached Fred's room, she released his arm with a squeeze and was about to carry on when Fred blurted out: "I've had an accident!"

Katya sensed immediately what type of accident it was. She could also tell from the desperation in Fred's eyes that he was upset and it had taken great effort to tell her.

"No problem at all, Mister Cox." She placed her hand on his shoulder reassuringly. "Accidents happen. Come, we'll sort it. It's no problem at all."

They entered Fred's room and Katya espied the pyjamas on the floor noting the staining.

"It's only leakage. We can sort that, no trouble at all." She gathered up the pyjamas. "Get dressed, Mister Cox and have some breakfast. I'll mop up shortly. No harm done, but if it's a worry for you, tell me, we can help. We have secret clothing, no one need know. Many people here have them. It's one of those things that happen as you get older. No worries." She walked to the door. "See you later, Mister Cox and don't worry."

Fred sat in the chair for a while wishing Josh was at the garden shed.

Fred breakfasted in silence. He was oblivious to the chatter and activity, even Jane could only elicit a few grunts. George accosted him with some repeated inane question but was ignored. It was left to Rita, shouting: "what's the matter with you, grumpy?" that drove Fred to his room.

Dinner followed in similar vein with the group talking amongst themselves. It was obvious to all that Fred was best left alone. He was wrestling with problems that perhaps only he could resolve.

In the afternoon a few visitors arrived. Albert, one of the dementia residents, was seated near Fred. His visitors, a son of retiring age and his wife, sat to one side. Albert could respond to some conversation with smiles and nods, if the conversation was appropriate to his condition. Spike, of course, was skilled at this. He could coax chuckles, nods and shakes of the head from him. Albert enjoyed the interaction and it obviously brightened his day.

His son sat quietly, but the wife was exuberant, loud, expounding to all and sundry about their holiday abroad. She ignored Albert and looked over the heads of nearby residents, as if playing to the gallery. She bragged. She affected a snooty voice and Fred, with his low mood, was irritated immediately.

"We flew out, you know. Oh no, not tourist class! Oh, the food, wonderful. We boarded the Ocean Leviathan at Miami. Outside balcony: marvellous! We ate regularly at Captain John's table, don't you know. But, would you believe, the highlight, the absolute highlight was when we docked in the Bahamas."

She spotted Fred looking at her and mistook his glare for enthralled interest. She concentrated on him as she continued. "We boarded a catamaran and guess what? She clasped her hands together and paused like a diva before delivering her masterstroke. "We swam with dolphins." She opened her hands wide as if waiting for applause.

There was silence, then a mocking voice, laced with sarcasm burst forth.

"Christ, I bet they were bloody thrilled. They must have been waiting all their bloody life for that event. What a bloody treat for them."

The woman was shocked into silence; eyes wide open, she stared at Fred.

Maurice stepped in to alleviate the situation. "Oh, it must have been wonderful. What an experience. A once- in- a- lifetime event, I wish I had witnessed it."

The woman smiled graciously at Maurice, his smooth tones soothing her hurt pride. She turned away from Fred and engaged with Maurice.

"God, it's a good thing Fred's not running the place. There'd be no clients here at all." Spike whispered to Lionel.

They watched as Fred rose and left the room. He looked sullen.

As Maurice engaged the woman in conversation, Jane couldn't help but notice, both Albert and his son had smiles on their faces.

"I think Fred's down in the dumps," George commented: "perhaps he's bilious." George surprised everyone with his comment. Normally he was limited to his repeated questions.

"He's certainly bilious all right. Most of the time, I'd say" Spike frowned.

"The man's got things on his mind. He's got to sort them out. It's the wrong time of life to be wrestling with problems," Lionel spoke quietly. "When you're facing your own mortality, you may look at yourself and not like what you see."

"Bit late in the day for that, I'd say," Spike sounded dubious.

"It's never too late to make amends and find a bit of inner peace. Let's hope he comes to terms with his demons." Lionel lapsed into silence, his face thoughtful.

14

Sunday dawned; a light drizzle fell from a dull grey sky. It landed silently on the lawn and drive. The morning was still, windless, leaves glistened. They moved only when tilting under the weight of water droplets. There was no birdsong: it was as if the still, wet morning had depressed and muffled everything.

Maisie, one of the cooks, shook off her brolly and entered the front door of The Laurels. "It's that wetting rain." She spoke with authority on the subject of rain.

"Morning, Maisie," Rose Richardson laughed: "I can see that."

Rose trotted briskly up the stairs to the nursing floor. She spoke with the night staff, assimilating information on the night's events. She greeted the morning team and discussed the day's priorities, trying to foresee any problems. The conversations were two-way, easy and unaffected. She spoke to her team as equals and was respected for it: she was in charge but rarely had a need to impose any authority.

Once she had done her rounds, spoken to patients and staff and satisfied herself as to their well-being, she descended to the ground floor. Apart from the usual routines and business of the day, she had a small concern.

Jane had come to her, last night, after tea: she shared her concerns over Fred Cox's state of mind and recent demeanour. Jane had developed a fondness for Fred. She was sure that beneath his abrasive manner and anti-social behaviour, there was a decent man. She liked his honesty and directness and sensed a sensitivity hidden and held in check.

Rose was concerned: she knew from day one that Fred was a complex man, struggling to come to terms with his situation. She understood human nature; physical and mental decline was a feature of most residents at The Laurels, it would arrive sooner or later. Some lucky individuals escaped that slow decline and held good health until their demise; for many, however, decline was slow and, particularly for their loved ones, painful to witness. Rose and her staff could cope with all that; that was their task. With the inevitability of decline, their duty was to comfort, cheer and afford sympathy and assurance to grieving relatives and friends.

People like Fred, however, were a challenge. Normal nursing and care could not resolve an unsettled mind: the best Rose and her team could do was to be available and sympathetic. Sometimes people had to heal themselves. She would speak to Fred later when the morning rush was over; she knew that as long as people like him mixed and didn't hide away, there was a good chance that group therapy could have beneficial effects.

Breakfast commenced. Fred, tetchy and somewhat withdrawn ate quietly, deep in his own thoughts. Once again, he missed his cigarette break with Josh. He had found comfort and an escape: satisfying his craving was only part of the benefit that he got from his thirty minutes with Josh.

After breakfast, Fred sat in the lounge reading the Sunday papers. Spike was laying into the Tories, reading out excerpts from his newspaper, hoping to goad Fred.

"More cuts on the way for the working class. Tax breaks for businesses. Tories say disabled to be humanely put down."

He added the last bit hoping to initiate a response from Fred, but he seemed oblivious. Fred viewed Spike as a left wing 'shit stirrer' and normally would have responded with his usual vigour. Today, though, he was withdrawn.

The group bantered amongst themselves, leaving Fred to his thoughts. As the mid-morning trolley came around with beverages, Maurice piped up: "Huh, huh. Who's arriving now? Looks like the mafia?"

Fred glanced up to see what the commotion was about. Through the window he could see two men emerging from a black limousine: one, middle-aged and one, older with a bald head.

"Oh Christ!" Fred groaned.

The others turned back to look at Fred. It was the first time he had responded to anything with any vigour all morning.

"Do you know them?" Lionel was intrigued.

"Bloody know them? They've come to bloody gloat!" Fred stared out of the window.

"Who are they?" Jane asked.

"Business rivals: Woodcock's Transport. Father and his weaselly bloody son, that's who. They've heard I'm in here and think they can muscle in on the business. Well, I'll tell you this much, they can kiss my bloody arse." Fred spoke vehemently, face red. "If they think they can get any change out of Mercedes, they can think again. She'll eat 'em for bloody dinner."

Mavis, one of the day girls walked in. "You've got two friends come to see you Mr Cox. Do you want to sit in the conservatory or dining room?"

"Friends? They're no bloody friends of mine. No, show them in here."

"We'll move away if you like Fred, if it's business," Maurice offered.

"Not bloody likely. Sooner they disappear through that door, the better."

In truth, he felt a bit vulnerable. He knew they wouldn't have come had they not thought him over the hill, ripe for the taking. Tough as he was, in his present state, he was unsettled and below par.

The two men walked into the lounge. They wore suits and ties and sneering grins, eyes scanning the room: they spotted Fred and walked over to the table.

"Well, Freddy boy, this is a nice surprise. Sad to see you've ended up in a place like this." The older man stood over Fred gloating.

Spike wheeled his chair to the side and invited the men to draw up chairs opposite Fred. They sat down at the table.

The weasel faced son grinned at Fred. "I'd have thought you'd have done better than this Fred; business not to good?"

Fred's anger rose. Just at that moment Mavis served tea and coffee to the table.

"Can I get you something, gentlemen?" she asked the Woodcocks.

"You certainly can, dear." Woodcock senior leered. "But first I'll have coffee, eh."

The pair chortled and guffawed, Fred was incensed.

"I expect the fragrant Mercedes is struggling a bit now Fred, eh? Maybe we could help out a bit." Woodcock junior smirked. "You obviously can't do much now Fred. Your time's come and gone."

Fred, face purple with rage, opened his mouth to respond. Instead of words, a coughing fit erupted. He struggled for breath, gasping. Then it happened. "God not now, please." Fred was desperate, the urgency overwhelmed him. He began to rise from his seat.

At that moment Rita, sitting against the rear wall with her daughter shouted out. "Why don't you fuck off? You are not wanted here!"

The Woodcocks turned, frowning, looking to see who it was.

At that moment, Fred stood: a spreading dark, wet patch appeared on the front of his light green slacks. It enveloped his trouser front and descended to his knees. He stood, mouth open, eyes wide, transfixed to the spot.

"You must excuse my mother. I never once heard her swear in sixty years. I am so sorry: I don't know what has happened to her." Rita's daughter was red faced with embarrassment.

Fred's group had witnessed everything and were mortified, desperate for something, anything to relieve Fred's predicament. The Woodcocks were about to turn round when Spike sprang into action. He overturned his coffee mug, spilling the contents across the table.

Maurice cottoned on immediately. "Clumsy devil, Spike. Hell's bells, you've soaked Fred."

Fred hadn't moved: he was still in shock.

Woodcock senior looked at Fred's soaked front and the spilt coffee.

"You've put yourself into a right place here, Freddy boy. Rather you than me."

Jane stood, taking Fred's arm. "No harm done Fred, it was only coffee. Come along, we'll get you cleaned up."

Jane led Fred, still in shock, out of the lounge. As they departed, the Woodcocks rose to take their leave. "I think we've seen enough, eh," the son smirked at his father.

"Please call again gentlemen, it's been a pleasure meeting you," Maurice smiled.

George drummed a dramatic riff on the table. As they turned to go, a bubbling sound rent the air and a familiar aroma wafted across.

"Oh dear," said Spike, "I think Jack's blockage has cleared."

The Woodcock's scuttled to the door.

"What a pair of slime balls. Good riddance." It was unusual to hear angry words from Spike.

"Poor Fred, I feel for him. That was a bad experience." Maurice looked round at the others, concern etched on his face.

15

Jane led Fred through the hall and down the corridor. Fred trailed Jane in a trance like state, the shock of his public mishap had numbed his senses; coming towards them was Katya. From a distance she could see Jane's concerned demeanour, the desperation in Fred's face and the wet patch on the front of his trousers. She looked, she analysed, she understood.

"Accident, Mr Cox? No worries." She spoke calmly with a cheery tone: "soon put things right. Let's get you to the bathroom."

As they approached the bathroom, Rose Richardson emerged from a side room. Again, immediately, she appraised and understood the situation. There was a need to act swiftly, she thought, before Fred's shock and humiliation turned to anger. Her experience told her there would be a kick back.

"Katya, would you fetch Mr Cox's dressing gown and some of our magic garments. We'll soon fix you up Fred," she spoke kindly. "These accidents happen: we all need a bit of help sometimes, don't we, Jane?"

Fred hadn't spoken till now but emerged from his shock defensive and angry. "I'm not wearing any of those bloody nappies." He was still distressed and looked appealingly at Rose.

"Now, Fred, there are worse things in life. Come on, we can tackle this problem. They're very discreet. Nobody need ever know."

"No, only the whole world and his bloody dog. Everybody saw it, especially that pair of bloody arseholes."

"No they didn't, Fred, only us, your friends." Jane pulled Fred round and looked him in the eye.

"Now look here." She spoke softly but firmly with a quiet determination "Nobody out there knows this." She pulled the waist band of her black trousers down slightly and revealed an elasticated top. She looked Fred in the eye. "There, I've told you and only you. Now do you understand?"

Fred was surprised, embarrassed even. He knew it had taken courage for Jane to reveal her problem. He was grateful. He looked into her eyes and calmed. He knew he had friends, but he was still bitter.

The incident passed but Fred didn't appear for dinner. Katya looked in and tried to persuade him: he accepted a couple of cheese and ham sandwiches and ate them in his room.

In the afternoon, Mercedes visited. Rose met her and explained quietly the week's events, Fred's difficulties and the embarrassing accident he'd suffered in public.

"Well, he's a proud man and bloody belligerent with it." Mercedes didn't hold back. "He's never had sympathy for others, so this is going to be difficult for him."

Rose felt Fred's desire to stay was in the balance and voiced her concern. "I was hoping he'd win through, but this traumatic episode has knocked him back. His group of friends covered for him. I feel sure nobody else realised. I don't think those business friends understood what had happened, fortunately."

"Huh, friends? I don't think so." Mercedes smiled grimly. "But, because it was them, it would have been much worse for him, a blow to his pride. Well, best go and see how he is. He's stuck it out longer than I expected." Mercedes grimaced at the prospect.

She knocked on Fred's door, paused and entered without any response from Fred.

"Hmm, it's you" was Fred's grumpy greeting.

Mercedes sat in the spare easy chair. Fred was sat in the other gazing out of the window.

"On your own?" The terse question didn't bode well, Mercedes thought.

"Yes, Lol's sorting out some emergency schedules for tomorrow." Mercedes explained.

"Can he manage it?" Fred asked sarcastically.

Mercedes ignored him, not wishing to get into conflict.

"So, come on Fred. How have you been?" she asked pleasantly.

"How have I been?" Fred's face reddened. "How have I bloody been? I've pissed myself in front of the Woodcock wankers, I'm wearing a bloody nappy and the office boy is running the business. How do you think I've been?"

Again, Mercedes bit her lip and let the slur pass.

Fred got angrier, face redder. "I'm washed up, stuck in this madhouse, nothing to look forward to except snuffing it. I've not even got grandkids. He couldn't even do that!"

That was it. Mercedes leaned forward, eyes blazing. "Right dad, I'm gonna tell you something."

Fred knew he'd gone too far. Mercedes never called him dad. He slumped back in his chair. Angry tears welled up in Mercedes eyes. She leaned forward and thrust her face nearer to Fred.

"Let me tell you, Lol always wanted kids, badly wanted kids, me too. Do you know why we've never had kids?" Her face was white with anger. "Do you know why?"

Fred was startled.

"It's because I couldn't have any. Not Lol. Me! I'm bloody barren!" She spat the words out. "Lol was disappointed, but he stood by me, loyal, a good man, but you never had a good word for him, never gave him any credit, no respect at all, even now. Without him, I'd have walked away from you and the business years ago because you're a bloody misery. When mother died you got even worse. No smiles, no thanks, no encouragement, no fun. Lol kept it all together. No matter how badly you treated him, he never said a bad word about you."

Years of pent-up anger and bitterness finally surfaced and Mercedes vented it on Fred.

"Let me tell you something else. You built this business from scratch. You devoted your life to it at the expense of everything and everybody. Who introduced the computer systems to cope with modern logistics? Who dealt with modern clients? Who smoothed the men when they were sick to the back teeth with your grumpiness? Who carried the business into modern times? You despised all that. The business would have gone without Lol. The days of your rough and ready methods, scribbling on the back of fag packets and kicking folks up the arse have gone. Now look at you, a bitter old man. You'll end your days a bitter old man. And who'll mourn you? Think about that. Have a good think about that."

Then she was gone.

Fred slumped, shocked. A coughing fit erupted and he fought for breath, pain gripped Fred's chest.

Across the hall in the lounge, Fred's small group had heard the raised voices. They had seen Mercedes stamp across the hall and out the door. They had seen her white, strained face.

"I think Fred's had a bad day, a very bad day. I wonder, will he be able to soldier on?" Maurice was pensive.

Fred lay on the bed, staring with blank eyes at the ceiling. He never emerged for the rest of the day. He refused any beverages and any offers of help; his mind was in turmoil. It was a jumble of unpleasant truths he wanted to shut out. He wanted it to end: he'd reached his nadir, his rock bottom. He could claw his way back or sink.

16

Dawn broke: the leaves on the cherry tree brushed gently on the window, the sun's rays had yet to rise above the perimeter wall and shrubbery. Birds heralded a new day and the house was quiet.

Fred lay, where he had lain all night, on his back, on top of the bed clothes, in his dressing gown. He still gazed at the ceiling. It was as if he hadn't moved all night: if he had dozed, he didn't know it.

He felt quieter, calmer, whether through exhaustion or laying to rest and accepting the previous day's events. In fact, he had reviewed his life, particularly his relationship with Mercedes. He had wrestled with his thoughts all night.

What sort of man was he? What sort of father was he? What had he achieved, other than the business? Why hadn't he paused to look at those near to him, or even himself? It had been uncomfortable: it was as if he had been sitting in judgement of himself and found himself wanting.

Fred rose from the bed and looked at himself in the mirror. His eyes were bleary and his heavy features drawn. He shaved, then walked across the hall, down the corridor, to the bathroom. It was quiet. In the bathroom he removed his dressing gown and his incontinence pants. He put them in a waste bin. His disgust had gone: there were more important things in life.

After showering he felt refreshed. He dressed, putting on a new 'nappy' and left his room. It was still early. He shuffled across the hall to the door with his stick. He stood for a while until Mandy, on night duty, spotted him.

"Dear me, Mr Cox, you're away early. Are you meeting somebody?" she smiled.

"You're dead right," Fred replied. "A foreigner."

His tone was almost jovial and Mandy laughed. She let him out the front door and Fred walked slowly to the side of the house. He paused at the corner looking up at sparrows squabbling under the eaves. The black and white cat approached and gazed up at him.

"What are you gloating at, cat?"

The voice was gruff, but the cat was tolerated. He walked slowly to the rear of The Laurels pausing again at the corner. He could hear activity from the kitchen. He proceeded along the path following its curves through the rear garden: the sun had climbed high enough to throw its light onto the garden; it looked fresh and bright with its various shades of green. Growth was lush with the late spring spurt. The morning freshness evaporated as the strengthening sun warmed the air. He rounded a curve and before him was Josh's shed.

Fred realised he was too early for Josh and leaned against the shed looking back towards the house. He spotted some dark birds hurtling around the house at high speed. They had thin, narrow wings and screaming calls. They twisted, skimming and disappearing around the corner of the house. He watched for some time, engrossed: focusing on them emptied his mind and with it some of the tension.

Fred had never bothered with gardens and nature. His house had been adjacent to his depot. The grounds, for what they were, merged into the yard of the garage. Fred's wife had a couple of window boxes, but that was it. When he moved to his flat there was a communal garden, but Fred never bothered with it.

He was still squinting at the aerial manoeuvres when Josh rounded the corner.

"Hey, Fred, what's this? Have you been up all night?"

"Come on: I've been waiting hours. I'm gasping." It was almost a plea from Fred.

Josh smiled. "Things must be bad, Fred."

He unlocked the shed, pulled out the old chairs and put his rucksack on the bench inside. He took out a flask and poured Fred a coffee in the flask cup. He reached up to a shelf and took down a battered tin mug for himself. There was no sugar in the coffee, but it tasted like nectar to Fred. While Fred sipped, Josh rolled two thin cigarettes. They lit up and savoured the moment.

After a peaceful interlude Josh turned to Fred: "well, Fred what's been happening in your life?"

Fred paused, drawing in a lungful of smoke. His hunched shoulders relaxed and he blew out the smoke slowly.

"I've lived through a bloody nightmare over the weekend." His words were slow and muted.

Josh passed no comment, allowing Fred to respond in his own time.

"I pissed myself yesterday in front of everybody." He paused. The rancour and bitterness of yesterday had left him and he spoke calmly. "I have to wear piss pants now."

Josh remained quiet, nodding along, face expressionless. There was a further pause while Fred drew on his cigarette.

"Then the daughter came to visit and I said some bad things to her, very bad. She told me some home truths. I bloody deserved it. I haven't been a very good father." Fred paused, looking at the ground.

A couple of minutes passed before Josh spoke.

"You know, Fred, my old man worked hard all his life. He never seemed to have any time for me and my brother. We were never close, he never played with us; it was just work and discipline. It was left to mother to rear us. I hated my father. Only after he died, when it was too late, did I realise he meant well: he thought it was the right way to rear us. He was wrong of course, I've tried to rear my kids differently; I've tried to involve them in activities. I've taken them to football, we've done things together. Of course, I haven't achieved much myself, but I don't regret it. Wealth's not everything."

Again, they sat quietly, sipping their coffee and savouring their smokes.

"You've still got time, Fred. You can put things right if you put your mind to it. Don't let things fester."

Fred nodded. He was leaning forward, his big hands hanging down between his knees, still gripping the nub end of his cigarette. After a pause, he pointed up to the house as half a dozen birds skimmed round the chimneys.

"They're swifts" said Josh gazing up. "They're like jet fighters. It's magic to watch them, they love whizzing round the house. Do you know; they come here, only to nest and rear their young? They then fly all the way back to Africa. They say they feed, drink and have sex on the wing: they never land except to nest. Every year they find their way back to the same place. That's dedication for you!"

Fred was impressed. Josh cleared the cups; their sojourn was over. He put the chairs away and Fred turned to go. Before he took his first step, Josh called out:

"Hey Fred, show me your pants before you go." Josh was grinning.

Fred pulled his waistband down and stuck his belly out.

"Oh yes," Josh enthused, "no need to be embarrassed about them, the height of fashion. You could be setting a new trend."

"Bollocks!"

17

The dining room was busy with the hubbub of breakfast activity. Fred paused at the door: he had rehearsed what he would say after yesterday's events. He was conscious of the way the group had rallied to help him, particularly Spike, whom he had maligned previously. Fred, never fully at ease in company, forced himself forward and walked directly to the table where the group sat. He paused, uncomfortable, unsure how to broach things.

George beat out a tattoo on the table with his cutlery. "It's Fred, he's back."

It was a welcome, as if Fred had been away and Fred was grateful for it. He nodded at George. He stood, holding the back of his chair. He looked across at Spike, struggling for words.

"I just want to say..." he faltered, his gruff features betraying the awkwardness he felt.

Spike saw his struggle and leaned forward. "No trouble Fred." He stretched out his arm to Fred with a closed fist.

Fred, initially confused, paused, then realised what it meant and butted Spike's fist with his own. The tension was gone. Fred breathed, relief written on his face.

"Come on, Fred," Lionel smiled, "we're all in this together."

"All for one and one for all!" Maurice held up his tea mug.

It seemed everyone was relieved. Fred's torment had been theirs. For the first time he felt at home, comfortable.

Jane squeezed his arm and looked across at him. Fred saw her smiling features, her mouth turned down slightly on one side, her eyes twinkling. Fred's face was rarely expressive, but Jane saw the subtle smile and thanks in his eyes.

"Let's have the full works," Spike thumped the table.

"Yes," said George, excitement on his face. "Has your bilious attack gone, Fred?"

"It bloody has and I'm having the full English and toast and jam."

"Yes, yes!" shouted George, drumming frantically on the table.

"Fred's paying, it's all on him." Spike was gleeful.

"All right, you scrounger. I'll pick up the bloody tab as usual."

The laughter was a release, a hurdle crossed, a barrier lifted.

"Don't be so noisy," Rita expressed her disapproval.

Fred gave her a 'thumbs-up' and a warm smile. Yesterday, she had helped him in her own inimitable way, although she may not have known it.

He gazed round the room: three elderly ladies sat together chatting. They wore their spectacles on the ends of their noses. They peered over the rims like wise owls. They added a certain gravitas to the dining room. At an adjacent table sat Cyril, Jack and Harold. All three were afflicted with dementia, yet sat nodding and smiling as if fully conversant with one another. Next to them were Emily and Joe, both Alzheimer victims. They sat with Mary: she, of course was immobile, other than her 'talking fingers' and eyes. Both these tables needed considerable attention. The staff bustled about attending and feeding. Rita sat with two other ladies in front of the window: she dominated, shouting out to anyone passing. Her remarks were often quite personal and the language fruity. Often the staff bore the brunt of caustic comments but they relished it. Rita was well liked and enlivened the proceedings. Eccentricities broke through any depressive atmosphere that might abound. They were a relief. Many residents remained in their rooms, taking their meals in private. Perhaps they felt secure there. Some didn't enjoy interaction with others.

Fred looked around his table. He viewed his companions with new eyes. He was fortunate: they were a good group, he wouldn't say so but they had carried him through a difficult time. George, who initially drove Fred to despair with his repeated questions, now accepted Fred as an old friend. His annoying repetition seemed to manifest itself with newcomers and visitors. He was a kindly man beneath the confusion.

Fred had also modified his judgement on Spike and Maurice. His views had moderated slightly, and he now accepted that not everything was black and white.

"How is everyone this morning?" Rose was relieved to see Fred at breakfast and leaned on the back of his chair.

He turned and gave a faint smile. It boded well, Rose thought, especially from an undemonstrative man like Fred.

It was left to Jane to give her the reassurance needed. "Pretty good, I think, Rose, pretty good."

18

One morning after breakfast, when the clatter of collected crockery and used cutlery had ceased, the gathered residents, who had the capacity to think ahead, settled into a discussion about the day's routine.

Maurice suddenly announced: "Hey, the Zumba girl's coming today, yippee!"

Fred gave a puzzled frown whilst some of his fellows shook their heads tutting.

Maurice explained: "She comes to exercise us Fred, to invigorate the aged."

"More likely to exterminate a few of us!

"Take no notice of Spike," Jane shook her head. "She comes, plays music and does a gentle exercise class. She's very good: it's well received and good therapy."

"You're always keen to go," Lionel nodded at Maurice.

"Yes, it's only because he fancies the instructor," Spike quipped.

"Well, she does move rather well." Maurice winked, suggestively. "Are you joining us Fred?"

"I'm bloody not."

The 'Zumba' girl duly arrived and set up in the dining room. There was a good turn-out. She was middle-aged, clad in black leggings and white top. She was friendly but efficient and soon organised her participants. Wheelchairs were placed at the front, the more able bodied behind and dementia-afflicted residents sitting against the wall.

Fred sat to one side: no amount of coaxing could persuade him to join the group. He couldn't understand why half the residents were there, many were immobile.

The girl, (everybody below sixty was called a girl), held up her hands and looked round the room at her charges. Their eyes followed her every movement.

"Right, everyone, let's begin." She played some slow, rhythmic music and began moving her hands and twisting her body. "Remember, everyone, just do what you're comfortable with."

Fred was astounded: the group seemed well-versed in the exercises and were soon following her every move, seated. One or two stood and performed more vigorously. The surprising thing, Fred noticed, were those demented, immobile residents. Their eyes were fixed on the girl and watched every movement. The normal blank look that many possessed was replaced with keen-eyed attention. The tempo changed progressively and the exercises became a little more vigorous.

The session was obviously well liked. Jane and Lionel sat with others, moving their arms and upper bodies, sometimes clapping with Fiona, the instructor. Many tapped their toes and even severely disabled people moved their hands or fingers.

Spike, sat in his wheelchair at the front, was encouraging those around him. He wiggled his fingers to set an example to the less mobile. He acted as interpreter between the instructor and his group. At the sides, standing, were some afflicted with Alzheimer's; many struggled with any communication, but seemed to respond to the music's beat and the movement of Fiona. They jigged and swayed with vigour. To one side, sat at a small table, was George. He strummed and tapped with his fingers on the table. Mentally he was part of a backing group of musicians. His hands were a blur on the table. He moved his fingers across the whole surface as if playing on a full drum kit. He was animated and completely engrossed in what he was doing.

Betty, from the kitchen, shimmied in, swaying her hips and moving her hands, flapper style. She sidled up to Fiona and whispered in her ear, never once losing her rhythm. After getting her reply, she turned for the door, still gyrating. She was large but moved well, Fred thought.

As she moved away, Spike shouted: "Give it some, Betty!"

Betty did a double shuffle and three pirouettes, before leaving the room.

Fred, although not participating himself and showing indifference, found it entertaining. The sight that dominated was Maurice. He was dressed in smart black trousers and a white frilled shirt. He was positioned at the side, in front of George's table. He danced dementedly with complete abandon. He wasn't even in time with the music, but threw himself round. He thrust out his hips and took exaggerated, ridiculous steps. He was puffing and panting and seemed to be trying to impress Fiona, who turned occasionally and smiled.

Fred thought it totally embarrassing. "What a prick. He'll bloody rupture himself, bloody show-off."

As the session drew to its conclusion, the music slowed. Fiona's actions slowed with the music and became gentler with less movement. The music faded and Fiona adopted a head up, relaxed position with slow shallow breaths.

"Wind down, everybody, wind down and relax. Empty your minds and close your eyes for two minutes."

There was complete silence broken at the end of two minutes by a huge snore from George, whose head rested on the table.

"You've relaxed George alright, Fiona. He'll sleep for a week," Spike jested.

"Where's the tea and biscuits?" Rita shouted.

Three elderly ladies rose from their seats. Jane had told Fred they always sat together and they were in their nineties, one ninety-eight. Two were widows and the eldest a spinster. She was a retired headmistress. Jane said she was a bit of a harridan and formidable. Maurice, apparently, called them the black widows and the headmistress, Miss Faversham.

As they passed Fred, one poked her stick at his midriff. "You could do with the exercise, young man," she frowned.

Fred glared at her.

"And don't give me that look!" she snapped, holding up her finger.

She then turned her attention to Maurice. "Why do you young people make such an exhibition of yourselves; in my day you would have been locked away for such behaviour, disgraceful."

"Maurice raised his hands in a cowed fashion, bowing low. "So sorry, ladies, I'll try to modify my behaviour."

They swept past heading for the tea trolley.

"Look at that." Maurice scowled. "If you got between them and the biscuits, you'd be trampled."

He turned his attention to Fiona. "That was wonderful, Fiona. I feel so much better for it." He unashamedly gushed and flirted.

Fred turned to Spike in disgust. "What's he in here for anyway? He seems able enough."

"He's a lost soul really." Spike spoke quietly. "He had stomach cancer, you know, and had some cut away. He couldn't look after himself, went to pieces. He's never married as far as we know, got no relatives. He can't cope with illness or problems, buries his head in the sand. He's a flirt and a ladies man but can't seem to form relationships. A bit pathetic, really. He rarely speaks of his past; he seems to have been a 'gopher' for some showbiz agent. Mind, you can't tell with Maurice. Is it true? Still, there's no harm in him."

"Hmm;" Fred watched Maurice preening and flirting with Fiona.

"You see, Fiona, it's pronounced 'Maureeeece. It's the French blood coursing through my veins. It reflects in my wild, passionate nature."

"Christ!" said Fred, loudly. He turned away: "I can't bear to watch."

"Who's blaspheming?" shouted Rita. "Wash your mouth out!"

19

It was a glorious morning; Fred sat with Josh, smoking and sipping coffee. Fred was attempting to coax the robin to feed from his hand. He had succeeded in getting the bird to feed at his feet, but had failed at the last hurdle.

"You know, Fred, he's beginning to accept you. You could become one of us, given time. We are all God's creatures, you know."

"Do you believe in that stuff?" Fred asked watching the robin hopping round his feet.

"Well, this is the way I see it, Fred, the missus believes and I couldn't argue with her. Nobody knows for sure."

Josh paused sucking on his roll-up. Fred leaned back. It was the closest Fred ever came to complete relaxation. Josh's thirty minutes had been Fred's salvation.

"I think the church does a good job except when the barm pots take over. They set good rules, The 'Ten Commandments' for instance, nothing wrong with them. They give folks a purpose and some comfort. But me..." Josh paused, "this is my thinking: when you're dead, your body, your spirit, whatever, begins new life. The cycle never stops. I heard Lionel talking once, he's a clever bloke. He said we have billions of molecules that fly off when we die. He said there are so many; we've probably all got a bit of Shakespeare in us."

"Shakespeare?" Fred was scornful.

"Well, maybe Attila the Hun, in your case."

"Balls."

"Anyway, the Rev. Tom comes round today. Have a word with him, he's a good bloke.

"Pfft!" Fred wanted no involvement with clergymen.

Dinner followed the usual routine. Fred was now well versed in The Laurels' ways. He was used to the eating arrangements and menus. He now tolerated the feeding habits of those round him. After dinner, Rose Richardson popped her head in the dining room.

"Is everyone ok?" She asked cheerily.

'Miss Faversham', who Fred now kept a wary eye on, beckoned with her finger to Rose, who obliged and joined her.

"No trouble at all Miss Lewis." Rose was saying. "We can sort that. I'll get Josh to look in later."

As she walked past Fred's table she gave a wink: "how about you lot, any problems?"

"No," said Lionel, "it was rice pudding today."

"Good old rice pudding," enthused George. "I had jam on mine."

"You have jam on everything," Spike commented.

"Yeees, jam every day: does you good. Raspberry's nice: mind, nothing wrong with apricot, or blackcurrant. No, nor strawberry, but raspberry's nice." George smacked his lips. He was easily pleased where food was concerned.

"Do you think George likes jam?" Spike jested.

"Does the Pope pray?" quipped Lionel.

"For goodness' sake don't run out of it, Rose, it would be disaster." Jane smiled at Rose.

"And how are you, Fred?" Rose asked, leaning over Fred's shoulder.

"Not too bad." That was about as good as it gets with Fred. Rose was satisfied: it had been a rocky road for Fred, but things were looking up, Rose thought.

"Rev. Tom will be bouncing in soon," Rose informed.

"Bouncing's the key word," Lionel jested "he's like an overgrown puppy."

"What's the betting he's got odd socks. Never mind, Fred, he'll smooth the way for you, especially if you donate to the bell fund." Maurice assumed a solemn face.

"Come on, you lot, you know he's a good fellow." Jane smiled.

Most residents retired to the lounge after dinner and were settling when Rev. Tom marched in. He was tall, over six feet, had a mop of brown curly hair, a toothy grin and thick framed specs. He was quite young. He was gangly, arms and legs everywhere. He marched into the lounge with huge strides, immediately tripping on a table leg.

"Afternoon, everyone," he boomed, his voice was loud and hearty.

"He can penetrate the deafest ear," Lionel whispered.

"You were wrong about his socks." Spike peered at the vicar's feet.

"Yes, but look at the shoes."

"They're both black," Spike observed.

"Yes, but look at the styles," Maurice persisted: "one's got a buckle and one hasn't. Told you!

Rita's raucous tones killed the discussion. "What's under your cassock, vicar?"

"Hello, Rita. How are you?" Rev. Tom boomed, totally unaffected by Rita's remarks. "You're looking very cheery today."

Rita giggled like a schoolgirl.

"And hello, ladies, so pleased to see you." Rev. Tom addressed the black widows. "How is your day?"

"Good luck with that," Fred growled.

"He's got them round his little finger," Jane whispered to Fred, "even Maurice has failed there."

Fred had a new-found respect for the vicar. The ladies were simpering over him. 'Miss Faversham' was brushing fluff off his cassock, fussing and tutting.

Rev. Tom was like a breath of fresh air. He worked the room with skill and compassion. His loud laughter ringing out, at other times he sat quietly with residents, comforting and allaying fears. He had the gift of communication, like Spike. He communed with those with limited, muddled or no conversation. Even badly demented residents smiled and nodded as if they were engaged in meaningful discussion.

"I'll give him his due," Lionel conceded, "even if he fails to save your soul; he'll cheer your way to hell and damnation."

"Uh oh, here he comes," Maurice hissed: "keep your feet under the table, or he'll tread on them."

"Oh, stop it!" Jane smiled: "I'll report you to Miss Faversham."

"Oh God no, anything but that."

"Afternoon, everyone: how's this little group today?" The vicar drew up a chair and sat down. He looked round the table spotting Fred. "A new face." He gave Fred a toothy grin.

Even Fred couldn't dislike Rev. Tom. He was open faced, open mannered and easy company.

"This is Fred," George chirped: "he gets bilious, you know."

"Pleased to meet you, Fred." Rev. Tom shook Fred's hand vigorously, laughing. "I hope your bilious attacks improve."

"You won't convert him, he's beyond redemption," Spike chirped.

"I'm not here to convert anyone," Rev. Tom laughed.

"Bit too late for me," Fred said quietly.

"It's never too late for anybody, Fred. Even if you don't want conversion, you can enrich your life and that of others. Even in mature years you can spread a little happiness, do a few good deeds, you'll be amazed how good it feels."

"I don't see Fred as a do-gooder," Maurice quipped."

"You don't have to be a do-gooder, or a God-botherer." Rev. Tom laughed at his own comment. "Ordinary folks can do extraordinary things. Give it a go, it feels good. When you are young, life's taken up, rearing children and scraping a living."

"Living a life of debauchery," Spike interjected pointing at Maurice.

"That too," Rev. Tom hooted, "but, with maturity, comes time for reflection and opportunity. Seize the day," he said dramatically, wagging his long forefinger. He stood to leave, knocking over his chair with a clatter. "Who put that there?" He adopted a comical exaggerated frown.

"You did vicar. Three hail Mary's!" Rita shouted.

"Thanks for telling me, Rita," he laughed, "but three 'hail Mary's' are Father Murphy's territory. I'll just say a little prayer."

With that, he swept out with a smile and a wave. He left everybody with a smile and a thought. Even Fred was thoughtful.

20

New arrivals at The Laurels inevitably, with time, slipped into its routines. There was a similarity to new pupils starting school. Initially, nervous apprehension, reluctance, even hostility might be evident, but slowly reluctance turned to acceptance and in most cases a comforting security. To the proprietor and staff however, maintaining comforting routines was a constant battle.

Rose Richardson sat at her keyboard typing. Her small office was situated at the back of The Laurels, next to the kitchen. Her face was contorted in a worried frown. Since Rose had employed some part-time help, her accounting and admin. improved one hundred per cent; nevertheless, balancing the books was a struggle. Regulations, inspections, recommendations, all resulted in higher costs. Her margins were small. For all the work she put in, the rewards, certainly, were not financial.

Last year, an elderly frail resident from upstairs, had somehow dragged herself from her bed, fell and broke her hip. The safety rail was down briefly, while Amy, the carer, changed her bed pad. She was a good girl, but in the couple of minutes it took Amy to fetch a new pad from her trolley, the accident occurred. It was, of course, deemed negligent and Amy was devastated. There was criticism of The Laurels and although Rose did her best to support and reassure Amy, she left and Rose lost a good girl. It was a constant struggle, providing a caring service, balancing the books and satisfying the authorities.

Rose envied the resources large companies had at their disposal. Few could match Rose's team for dedication and care, but the dice seemed loaded against small concerns.

Rose sighed, rubbed her forehead and gazed from the window. It was a fine morning. Rose spotted Josh tying back some rambling rose branches. For a minute Rose envied him. He was a good chap, versatile and able to tackle anything, but oh, for a bit of that freedom. Rose knew he wasn't well paid, but thankfully he loved the work and was rock solid.

There was a knock and Betty, the cook, put her head round the door with a concerned look on her face. "Maisie's been called out; her daughter's had an accident. She's had to go and pick up her granddaughter."

"Oh dear: hope she's ok. Can we cope?"

"Yes, we'd got everything prepared for dinner. If Mavis can give me a hand, we can manage."

"Thank goodness for that. Thanks, Betty." Rose ran her fingers through her hair. There would be another staff shortage soon. Denise had broken a tooth that morning and needed emergency treatment. "Ah well," Rose sighed, "such is life." She knew it was manageable: she could step in, a shortage downstairs wasn't critical. A knock on the door relieved her thoughts. It was Jane. "Come in, Jane: have a seat."

Jane, limping slightly, stepped into the room.

Rose always found Jane 'easy'. She was inevitably good humoured, easy to talk to and was a good listener. Jane had been a wonderful pianist and would often sit down at the old piano in the hall and play. The residents loved it. She played light classical and some popular rollicking tunes. Since her stroke, however, she hadn't played. She had recovered well. Her mouth, of course, had a slight turn-down and she limped slightly. The stiffness in her arm had much improved. Rose felt she could play, but pride in not attaining her previous high standard prevented her.

Rose had asked Jane to pop in. Mercedes had previously phoned Rose, concerned about her father. She was busy all week and after her confrontation with Fred decided not to visit on the Sunday. She told Rose she would let him stew a bit. Fred was never good company. He never seemed bothered if Lol and Mercedes visited, even when he resided in his flat. Even so she was concerned.

Rose filled Jane in on Mercedes' concern and her confrontation with her father. Jane was aware of the row. Quite a bit of it had been audible in the lounge, on the day.

"What do you think, Jane? Is Fred ok?" Rose enquired.

Jane paused a moment before responding.

"I see a change coming over Fred: he's listening more. He's not so self-absorbed. He's observing others. He's still the gruff Fred, of course, but he seems easier in his mind. I think he's going to be fine. He's not sulking, as men sometimes do." Jane and Rose both sniggered. "It certainly won't hurt him if Mercedes misses a visit. I think she'll notice a difference when she next comes."

"Good." Rose was heartened. "I feel the same way myself."

Mavis tapped the door. It was the tea trolley. Rose invited Jane to stay and have a cuppa and talk about men. The tone was light-hearted: it cheered them both.

Jane had just left Rose's office when Mandy rushed in without knocking.

"I think we've got an inspection." She was breathless. "A car's drawn up: looks official."

"Oh no;" Rose stood up, face strained. "It's going to happen again. Oh dear. Quick, run and tell Katya we are one short. You will have to do your best."

Rose phoned, warning upstairs of the forthcoming inspection. She knew the team would put on a good show. Thank heavens the paperwork was up to scratch. They were one down in the kitchen and short on the ground floor. She knew she wouldn't be able to cover while an inspection was in progress.

She rushed into the kitchen. "Mavis, back to your post quickly, inspection!"

"Oh dear;" Mavis ripped off her whites and shot out the door.

"Noo, couldn't be worse, Mrs Richardson." Betty looked concerned.

"Plan B." Rose rushed to the window. She flung it open and shouted Josh, beckoning frantically. Josh, sensing an emergency, ran to the rear kitchen door.

"Quick, wash your hands and get your whites on: you're Betty's assistant."

Josh looked puzzled, but didn't question it.

"Can you cope, Betty?" Rose put her hands on Betty's shoulders.

"Yeees," Betty was calm. "I'll soon have Josh up to speed. You get off and don't worry."

Rose left. She felt confident that Betty, with Josh's help, would cope. She bustled into the hall as Mavis opened the door to the Care Quality Commission inspectors.

Rose knew they would be present during dinner, one of their busiest times. She was a man down and likely to be criticised and receive an 'Improvement required' tag. It couldn't be helped, they would just have to do their best, but it was disappointing after all their good work. She sighed, resignedly, and walked over to greet the inspectors.

Meanwhile, in the lounge, Katya was rallying everybody.

"Listen up, everybody, do your best, best behaviour, we've an inspection any minute. It's looking bad for The Laurels because we're short staffed. That's very bad. Mrs Richardson has worked so hard, we all have." Katya's face was etched with disappointment.

"Can't we do anything to help?" Spike spoke up.

"We can all help out a bit," chipped in Lionel.

"I know everyone will help," Katya said gratefully, "but it's a staff member we need. I am afraid you are all a bit too old," she said sympathetically.

"Maurice is not, and he's not disabled yet."

"I can't do it, no way!" Maurice protested. "Not me!"

"Course you can. Come on, make an effort! You owe the place."

"Don't care. I can't do it." Maurice shook his head vigorously.

"Come on, young man, get off your bottom. It will quell some of that wayward energy you possess."

Maurice looked across towards the 'black widows', startled.

"Come on, Maurice: you can do this." Jane appealed to Maurice.

After a pause and a big sigh, Maurice conceded, "Oh alright."

"Yes." Shouted George.

"Quick, I'll get you a tabard. Just do your best and attend to people. Everybody will help you." Katya bustled out, returning with a navy-blue tabard. Maurice donned it fussing over the size.

"Well, you do look dinky," Spike tittered.

"If I hear any more, I won't do it."

"You look very professional," Jane soothed, "more like a Doctor, I'd say."

Maurice puffed up at this, preening a little.

"Here they are," hissed Lionel.

A man and woman walked in, their eyes scanning all and everything. At that moment came the call to dinner. Residents started to move to the dining room, Maurice amongst them.

"Not you," Spike snapped, hand shielding mouth. "You've got to help everybody. Just do what Katya is doing."

Maurice turned and guided one of the residents towards the dining room. He could feel the inspectors' eyes scrutinising him. Jane took the hand of Albert and between them they herded everybody into the dining room.

"Where's me dinner?" Rita piped up.

Lionel poked Maurice, who jumped forward to pacify her. "It's coming Rita, just be patient."

"I want jam on mine," George chirped.

"No, that's for dessert, George." Maurice beamed at the inspectors, adopting a superior manner. He was relishing his newfound authority.

Soon dinner was served. Josh had performed admirably under Betty's tutorage. The woman scrutinising them seemed pleasant. Betty thought things were going well.

"No cock-ups, up to now," she whispered to Josh. Tell your wife, she's done a good job."

To get a few kind words from Betty was praise indeed. Josh was pleased.

Back in the dining room, Maurice was spooning jam sponge and custard into Mary's mouth. He was beginning to struggle a little. He hadn't signed up for this, he thought. He copied Katya, spooning, wiping and picking up cutlery off the floor.

"It's like the Mad Hatter's Tea Party," he thought. "I can't bear it."

But bear it he did. Things were going well until Katya pushed a wheelchair bound lady to the toilets. Maurice was now on his own.

Rita suddenly piped up. "He's not a carer. He's Maurice."

The stern-faced inspector turned to Rita.

"Course he is, Rita. He's the best," Spike intervened.

"Liar, liar, your pants are on fire."

A familiar gurgling assailed their ears and a noxious odour pervaded the air.

"Jack's crapped in his pants," shouted Rita.

All eyes turned to Maurice, who had visibly paled. He looked round desperately for Katya.

"Come on, man, you've got to act," Spike hissed. "The inspector's watching: take him to the toilet."

Maurice moved forward gulping air and gritting his teeth. Feigning indifference, he said, with authority: "come along Jack, let's get you sorted." He took Jack's arm and led him out into the hall and down the corridor. The inspector followed him out. All the time Maurice hoped and prayed for Katya to appear: surely she would.

They reached the bathroom door. Maurice turned desperately, but Katya was absent. The inspector was still there.

"You'll have to help me, you know." Jack pleaded plaintively.

With one last look, Maurice entered the bathroom with Jack. The inspector, obviously satisfied, spotted Rose and accompanied her upstairs.

The dining room had emptied and Spike and the group had anxiously filtered out into the hall. They watched the inspector ascend the stairs with Rose.

Lionel expressed everyone's concern "I hope we've carried it off."

"I think Maurice did very well," Jane asserted.

Just at that moment, loud retching sounds echoed along the corridor. Katya had just returned from attending to Emily and paused at the bathroom door. She opened it as Maurice lurched out, handkerchief to mouth, face white, eyes streaming.

"Oh dear God; oh God!" He staggered down the corridor to his room.

For a moment the group were stunned, then, Spike and Lionel burst out laughing. Spike had tears running down his cheeks and Lionel was biting his fist. Jane tried her best not to laugh, but it was infectious, even Fred was grinning.

"Was it the colour or the texture that upset Maurice?" Spike asked with a serious face.

"Well, I don't think he likes khaki," Lionel responded with an equally serious face.

They started again: the corridor rang with helpless laughter.

At tea, everybody was gathered in the dining room: Rose walked in with Josh and Betty and any staff who could be spared.

"I would just like to say a few words to everybody. You all know we had an inspection today. It could have been disastrous, but you were wonderful. Thank you so much."

Rose's voice faltered slightly. Suddenly the whole room erupted into applause. As the applause died, Maurice appeared. He hadn't been seen since his ordeal earlier. Cheering and clapping greeted his arrival. He looked startled.

"Well done." Rose hugged him: "you were a wonderful carer. Thank you."

Maurice flushed and smiled.

"He's not a carer. He's Maurice," Rita shouted.

"You're correct, Rita, I am not a carer. I am Maurice, but I take my hat off to all you carers. More power to your elbow and long may you flourish.

21

Fred and Josh were discussing kids.

"They need a good kick up the backside. They have things too easy." Fred got into his stride. "When I was a kid you got nowt, sweet F.A. You had to work for it: I delivered papers at night and groceries at the weekend on a bloody old bike. Even then, my mother had most of it. Look at 'em now: computers, tablets, iPhones and they do nothing. What's the world coming to?"

Fred broke off and puffed his cigarette: they sat in silence for a while, Josh digesting Fred's observations.

"Yes, but Fred, the world has changed: health and safety have killed kids' jobs. I used to help out on a milk round; we jumped off and on the back of a moving truck. We were outside the whole time; there was nothing to amuse you in the house.

"Yes." Fred grew nostalgic: "bread and jam, lived on it: sometimes bread and dripping. We'd be out shovelling up horse shit for the rhubarb: if the cat brought in a young rabbit, my mother would be after it for the stew. We never moaned or snivelled, just got on with it."

Josh grinned and sipped his coffee: "sometimes you need a bit of luck in life, a bit of a leg up."

"There's no luck," Fred exclaimed: "you make your own luck. It's your own effort, your own hard graft, if you wait for things to drop into your lap, you're a waste of bloody space. That's the trouble these days; people want the state to bail 'em out." Fred sucked hard on the nub end of his cigarette causing a coughing fit.

"Maybe," Josh was thoughtful, "but not everyone's got your drive, Fred. One thing has improved, we now know about the dangers of smoking."

"Too right," Fred concurred: "should have told me when I was ten, too bloody late now."

"Have you seen your daughter?" Josh enquired cautiously.

"Mmm," Fred mumbled, "I think things are a bit better."

The sound of an engine, roaring and splattered gravel broke their reverie.

Fred scowled: "it's that arrogant sod who brings Katya."

"Yes, he's a bad 'un," Josh agreed:" I don't know why she bothers with him."

"I worry about that girl," Fred frowned.

Josh noted Fred's concern. He knew from day one that Fred had a soft spot.

After mid-morning tea, a few visitors arrived. The more able residents generally welcomed visitors, but for those visiting demented relatives, the outcome could be upsetting.

Spike was sitting with Mary: he had been coaxing her to communicate with her fingers. She was almost completely immobile, but Spike had persevered and had succeeded in teaching her to raise her fingers for 'yes' and lower them for 'no'. He was practising the technique when her daughter arrived for a visit.

Spike welcomed the daughter who he had seen many times: "I've been talking to Mary, haven't I?" Spike said, looking at Mary.

Mary, hand resting on her wheelchair, raised a finger.

"You see," Spike explained to the daughter, "that means yes; now, Mary, do you like dogs?" The fingers pointed down: "what about cats?" The fingers pointed up.

The daughter watched with amazement: "well, I don't believe it, that's wonderful, mother."

Spike wheeled his chair away and said, "give it a go: see how you get on."

He joined the group at the table and engaged in a game of draughts with Lionel. From time to time he looked round to observe Mary and her daughter: they looked to be getting along well. The daughter was leaning towards Mary; Spike could see her fingers moving up and down. As simple and limited as it was, Spike's efforts had opened a new dimension to their relationship; Spike was quietly pleased with his efforts.

Across the room, Joe was sitting with his daughters and a son-in-law. They worked hard trying to elicit a good response from him. At first, he nodded along with their efforts, smiling occasionally: one of the daughters then showed him a photograph.

"Look dad, a photo of Mum: she looks very nice, doesn't she? It was at your retirement party, do you remember?"

Joe's demeanour suddenly changed: "I don't know her. Who is she? Don't come telling me, I don't want you here. Get out!" He became agitated and aggressive.

The daughter, a woman in her sixties was shocked. Her face reddened and she looked distraught.

"I'm sorry, dad, I didn't mean to upset you: I thought you'd be pleased to see the photo."

"Get out, get out and don't come back!" In his anger, Joe was lucid: his speech was clear and sharp contrasting with his usual garbled and disjointed phrases.

The other daughter jumped to her distressed sister's aid.

"Now, dad, there's no need to be nasty, Karen was only trying to cheer you up."

"Get out, get out, you're trying to rob me!" Joe was shouting.

The son-in-law tried to calm him but to no avail and they were forced to stand and walk away. One daughter was crying and upset; the other held her arm and guided her to the door. As they passed, Jane put her hand on the distraught woman's arm.

"Don't take it to heart, he doesn't know what he's saying," she spoke kindly.

"He used to be so kind and gentle," the daughter wept: "I can't bear it."

"It's not your dad as you knew him, it's that horrible disease: he can't help what he says. Remember how he was, not how he is now: that was your real dad."

The daughters couldn't speak, but mouthed a silent thanks; grateful for Jane's kind words. The son-in-law paused and expressed his gratitude, "thank you, it can be upsetting for the girls; sadly, he's not the dad they knew.

They walked out and Spike wheeled his chair up to Joe. "Hey up, Joe, how are you doing?"

He beamed at Spike: his mood had changed in the blink of an eye.

"Do you know; we may not think it, but we are the lucky ones in here; it's so distressing to witness sons and daughters unrecognised and disowned by their parents. I dread the thought of what the future may bring."

Jane's observations and fears were shared by all. Most had come to terms with their mortality, but the manner of their passing weighed heavily: mostly, it was a subject unspoken.

22

Before dinner, Mavis reminded everybody: "don't forget, the Brownies are coming this afternoon. They're singing a few songs and collecting a bit of money for their summer camp."

"Oh, they're lovely," said Jane: "so sweet. They do brighten everyone."

After dinner most residents gathered in the lounge, a few in the hall. At two-o-clock precisely, Mavis opened the front door to the Brownies. They marched in by twos, 'Brown Owl' leading the way. There were about twenty of them all looking rather proud. They gathered in the hall, sitting cross-legged so everyone could see them. A plump lady in uniform sat down at the piano.

"Good afternoon, everyone, we've come to sing a couple of songs for you and hope it will cheer your day."

After Brown Owl's introduction, she raised her hands and the girls sang 'Over the Hills and Far Away.'

Fred had retired to his room: He always shied away from children, especially if it involved anything emotional. He kept his door open though and peered out from within.

One of the older girls recited a poem, hands behind back, turning her head from side to side, with total confidence.

The residents were enraptured with the Brownies. Music and children always captured their attention: they watched avidly, enchanted.

They sang songs from modern stage shows, their voices gaining in strength as their confidence grew. When they received applause, they flushed with pride turning to one another giggling. They looked smart in their yellows and browns. Fred noticed the pianist bounced up and down on the piano stool in time to the music. She gazed round, beaming at everybody.

At the end of their show they received rapturous applause. Jane Richardson stood in front of them and proffered thanks. She leaned forward and looked around at each Brownie, as if personally thanking each. She had that easy way that some possess with children. Fred, hiding in the shadows, wished he was at ease in a similar way: he didn't know how to cope with children.

"The Laurels have loved having you here and here's a little donation to your summer camp," Rose smiled at everyone.

She turned to the residents: "if anyone would like to donate a bit of spare change, the girls will come round with a bucket. Don't worry if you have none; the girls won't mind."

Fred watched three or four of the girls bustling excitedly with their buckets. A lot of the residents were fiddling for loose money. He saw Spike put a note in the bucket and whisper to the girl. She was eight or nine with long, black hair. Tossing her hair over her shoulder, she turned on her heel and skipped across the hall towards Fred's door: Fred leaned back trying to be inconspicuous. It was to no avail; the girl tapped the open door and skipped in.

She flicked her hair back, her bright dark eyes perusing Fred and weighing him up. Having assessed him, she stood, holding her bucket in front of her and addressed him. Her eyes were wide but fixed on a point somewhere over Fred's shoulder: she showed no fear of the grumpy Fred.

"That man, over there, said to go and see Mr Frederick," she spoke rapidly, barely pausing for breath. "You see we're collecting for summer camp: it costs a lot of money, you know, but you don't have to give anything. Mrs Belshaw said we are not to pester people.

I've just got my camping badge, you know." She pointed to a badge on her arm proudly, pursing her lips. "I've got four badges now, my friend Victoria has got six, but I'm catching her up. She's got a badge for first aid and kindness to animals. I've got a budgerigar, you know: he's blue. I can do the splits, shall I show you?"

She put her bucket down and slid into the splits on the floor. She jumped up flushed with success, watching Fred out of the corners of her eyes.

"My dad's a lorry driver, you know." She tossed her head back, flicking her hair over her shoulders. She fidgeted all the while, striking poses, feet turning this way and that.

"I might get another badge for being kind to old people."

Fred sat open mouthed. The girl had spoken more in two minutes than he had all day.

"Who does your dad work for?" he asked finally.

"Fred Cox Transport," she answered importantly.

"Oh," said Fred.

"Yes, mum said dad should ask Mr Cox if he could borrow some transport. We need to take our camping stuff to Wales for summer camp. Dad said that Lord Fred would have his guts for garters if he asked."

"Oh," said Fred.

"Anyway, I've got to go now: you don't have to give any money, bye." She turned and skipped across the hall; Fred leaned to the side watching her go.

Ten minutes later Mrs Belshaw, 'Brown Owl', was gathering her excited charges together, ready to leave.

The young girl with dark hair glanced across towards Fred's door and waved. The 'kindness badge' was in her thoughts. She saw a big hand beckoning her in the doorway: she skipped across.

Fred stood back in his room: as the girl approached he handed her a piece of paper.

"Tell your dad to speak to Lol about some transport for camping. Don't forget."

"Ok, Mr Frederick, I will; thank you."

She skipped back to Brown Owl and handed her the paper. Brown Owl's eyes widened and she hurried over to Rose

"Oh, Mrs Richardson, I can't accept this. It's too much. He probably doesn't know what he's doing."

Rose looked at the cheque, a smile on her face.

"Oh, I think he certainly does: don't worry, it will be fine."

"I must go over and thank him." Mrs Belshaw was grateful but flustered.

"No, I don't think he'd want that: he's a private, modest man. It's ok."

Fred watched the Brownies troop out. As 'his' little girl crossed the hall she waved vigorously to him. He gave a self-conscious wave back.

After they had left, Fred sat, a hint of a smile on his face, as he recalled the girl's conversation. The smile broadened to a silent chortle.

Later, sat at tea, Jane was discussing the Brownies' performance.

"They were so keen to perform and please. It was a pleasure to see them. It's so nice to have young people around, it lifts your spirits."

"Takes your mind off death and dying," Lionel commented

"I'll tell you what, Fred; that little tinker with the black hair was a live wire. I saw her bounce across to your room," Maurice commented.

"She certainly was." Fred's smile surprised everybody: "she certainly was."

23

The Laurels' guests were breakfasting. Amongst the clatter of cutlery and the bustling of staff, murmured conversation could be detected. For most however, eating was the priority. Suddenly and sharply, a raucous voice cut through the air causing all but the most dedicated diners to look up.

"My friend wants to come in here," Rita shouted out, "but I told her, somebody's got to die first!"

The diners, at the breakfast table, paused: George hummed a funeral march, his face solemn. The 'black widows', although well used to Rita's outbursts, frowned and tutted, shaking their heads.

"It certainly won't be one of them," Maurice whispered vehemently: "they'll live to at least hundred and twenty."

"I'll tell you what, Rita, we'll draw lots for it." Spike held his finger up: "whoever draws the short straw snuffs it and your friend takes their place."

Rita cackled gleefully.

"Dear God," Maurice conjectured, "is that what it comes to, the world waiting for you to die? God preserve us."

It was Lionel's view that the world considered them expendable, their opinions worthless, their accumulated wisdom disregarded. The fact that they had lived, worked, loved, was forgotten.

"Well, I'll tell you now," Maurice spoke earnestly, "I'm not finished yet, I'm not ready to throw in the towel: I've still got some sap and it still rises. You lot can sit and vegetate but count me out." He threw his head back, aquiline features still handsome, greying hair still thick. He rose from the table; as he crossed the room, he paused near the door.

Sitting, writing on a clipboard was Abbey, a college trainee. She was gaining work experience in social care. She had been at The Laurels for a week and had been received very favourably. The staff and Jane Richardson couldn't praise her enough: she was dedicated, caring and shied away from no task. Everybody commented on her pleasant personality, she was inevitably smiling and compassionate. She was also attractive: flawless complexion, large eyes and curvaceous figure.

Maurice had been ogling her all week, pouring on the charm, holding doors open for her, enquiring about her studies. He had observed her taking some of the less able residents to the bathroom for showers and baths: from this he had hatched his plan. He leant on Abbey's chair, struggling for breath, shoulders slumped.

"Whatever's wrong?" Abbey looked up at him, concern on her face.

"I am not so good, today," Maurice's mouth sagged and his breathing was laboured. "I couldn't manage to shower this morning." His voice was weak and hoarse: "I'll try again after dinner, I just feel so weak and I feel terrible without a shower."

"We can't have that, if you can't manage your routines, your well-being suffers." Abbey's face had a worried frown: "after dinner, if you are still struggling, I'll help you."

Maurice thanked her sorrowfully and limped out the door.

Fred had been watching him: "that lecherous bugger's up to something." For all his roughness, Fred always treated women with respect and propriety. Down at the transport yard, Fred would not tolerate any lewdness, especially around Mercedes. The men knew better than to speak coarsely of women if Fred was about.

"I think he's desperately trying to thwart ageing," Lionel theorised: "he has been a swashbuckler in his time but now he can't face the inevitability of decline. In fact, he can't face anything unpalatable."

Fred was disgusted, declaring Abbey a nice girl. He thought she might be a bit naive where bullshitters like Maurice were concerned.

"He won't do any good there," Spike concluded, looking across at Abbey: "she'll be fine, you'll see."

It was the weekend and at elevenses a few early visitors rolled up: Fred was surprised to see Mercedes and Lol walk in. Mercedes had been once since their confrontation, there had been a slight atmosphere, but the meeting had been civilised.

Today, Lawrence was his normal, easy-going self. Business was discussed; Fred was interested and keen and seemed less critical than normal. They covered goods, maintenance, contracts, manning: they discussed drivers and schedules and particularly the trucks themselves, Fred's favourite topic.

Lawrence was easy to talk to, unlike Fred and Mercedes who were sparing with conversation. He brought fresh interest to Fred's routine. There were never any long silences when Lol was present: he could switch topics easily and always listened to Fred's point of view with interest and good humour, even if he disagreed. This contrasted to conversations between Fred and Mercedes, which inevitably ended with some disagreement. Mercedes had been right: her assertion, that Lol was their saving grace, was probably correct.

Fred observed Lawrence with new eyes and a new-found respect. He listened to him without butting in, he made no disparaging or cutting remarks: it was probably the longest conversation he'd had with him.

Mercedes was secretly delighted, pleased, that after all these years, Lol was getting the respect he deserved. There was definitely a change in Fred. It wasn't just because of their confrontation; The Laurels had also had an influence: he was less grumpy; she had never seen him so relaxed.

When they rose to leave, Mercedes turned to Fred: "do you know anything about John Edwards? He came to see us about some transport for the Brownies?"

Fred denied it, but Mercedes knew he probably did, but said nothing: she found it hard to believe that he had suggested an approach to Lol.

As they turned to leave, Fred squeezed Mercedes' arm affectionately: then held out his arm, fist clenched, to Lawrence. There was a moment's puzzlement before Lol understood and reciprocated. They butted fists: it was a simple gesture from Fred, certainly never experienced before and Lol was taken aback. Mercedes felt a bit emotional.

As they walked to the car, Lol turned to her. "Are they feeding him happy pills? You know, Mer, I might just have finished my apprenticeship after thirty years!"

They burst out laughing; Mercedes linked her arm in Lol's. They walked, gazing at each other like young lovers.

After dinner, many residents dozed: full stomachs and tiring bodies combined to produce the afternoon torpor. Some retired to their rooms, some dozed in the easy chairs, so powerful was the desire to sleep, that heads lolled to the side or flopped down, chins resting on chests. It was reminiscent of childhood when small children dropped to sleep anywhere, in any position.

Advancing age, thinner skin and shrinking face muscle, endowed an ugly aspect to many sleepers. Cheekbones were more pronounced, noses and ears seemed larger, mouths dropped open. One or two residents had abandoned their teeth: if a snore disturbed them, mouths would chomp, noses meeting chins.

Spike, Fred, Lionel and Maurice were sitting at a table: Jane was sitting behind talking to 'Miss Faversham'. George dozed in his chair: mouth open, an occasional snore jerking his head.

"What a depressing sight; slow, protracted decline. I can't face any of that: before I get too decrepit, I shall end it all," Maurice looked round, a resolute look on his face.

"The only certainty in life is death," Lionel mused: "you can't book a slot, you know. Of course, one or two lucky people may choose their time, but they're few in number: most of us have to wait and suffer."

"I won't wait. I'll be one of those that choose," Maurice spoke with conviction.

"How can you do that?" Spike queried.

"Mark my words, I won't linger. Anyway, I'm weary of this talk and the sight of cadaverous snoozers. I'm looking for some good cheer, some young company; interaction with younger blood. I need a sympathetic and welcoming shoulder, someone with an appreciation of elegance and breeding." Maurice fixed his eye on Abbey who was guiding Mary back into the room. "I leave you lot to decay slowly."

As he stood, he slumped and limped.

"Look at that, the brazen fraud," Fred exclaimed.

Maurice approached Abbey leaning on the wall as he did so: the trio could see him mumbling to her.

"Why, of course, of course I'll help you. Why don't you go along to the bathroom? Get yourself ready and I'll come along and assist you." Abbey smiled sympathetically at Maurice, her big eyes shining.

Maurice, with a pained face, nodded his thanks and limped towards the door giving the trio a triumphant grin as he went.

"That's never right," Fred fumed, "I'm going to have a word with that girl."

"Leave it," Spike held up his hand to Fred, "see what happens: it'll be resolved, you'll see".

Rose Richardson appeared, striding across the room, carrying ledgers: Abbey approached her, pointing to the departing Maurice and explaining to Rose her intentions.

"Oh, I see, Abbey. We must help Maurice, but I've got an important job for you upstairs."

She walked back to the door with her arm round Abbey's shoulders explaining her task. After a couple of minutes, she returned and approached Mandy who had been attending Albert. Rose, normally very discrete, spoke loudly: "apparently he needs help showering; he's not up to it today, seemingly."

Mandy, interpreting correctly, also spoke loudly. "Oh dear, oh dear, we can't have that, Mrs Richardson: I must go along and help him immediately."

Mandy rolled up her sleeves revealing her ample forearms: she had an array of tattoos from wrist to elbows. She nodded her head at Rose, slowly and deliberately, "leave it to me." She marched towards the door.

"Ho, ho: now the fat's in the fire!" Lionel chortled.

"All Maurice's dreams and fantasies are coming true," hooted Spike. "Quick, into the hall, we are going to miss the fun."

Even Fred was enthused: he and Lionel followed Spike in his wheelchair. They moved into the corridor near the bathroom door as Mandy closed it: they acted as if they had just met and stopped for a chat, they assumed a nonchalant, casual manner, all the time straining their ears.

"Oh, oh, it's you, Mandy." Maurice spoke faintly from the bathroom, a trace of panic in his voice.

"Oh dear, Maurice: not able to manage your shower, eh? Goodness me, we'll soon sort that. Let's be getting you in here, I bet you're upset, missing your shower." She spoke loudly, with authority and a slight hectoring tone."

"Well, I, hmm."

Outside, the eavesdroppers sensed Maurice's increasing apprehension and panic: they smirked at each other.

"In you go: let's be having you!"

"Ooh, it's a bit cold!"

"Come on, come on, don't be a wimp. Shall I do your bits, Maurice?"

"Oh no, no! I think I can manage, thank you," Maurice's voice became squeaky.

"I'll tell you what. You do your bits and I'll do your back. And you know, where the sun doesn't shine."

"Oh! Oh!"

Outside, Lionel and Spike were almost wetting themselves with laughter. Fred, not known for his laughter, chortled to himself, inducing a coughing fit.

Rose Richardson walked across the hall: "what are you lot up to?"

"Nothing: just laughing at Fred's joke," Spike spluttered as they headed back to the lounge.

Rose smirked, knowingly: she had doubts about Fred cracking jokes.

At tea, Maurice appeared in the dining room; he was subdued and sat quietly: he looked around sheepishly. When tea was over, Spike casually turned to him.

"Oh, by the way how did you get on with Abbey and your shower, everything ok?"

"Mmm, not bad, pretty damn good in fact."

"Did you get some personal treatment?"

"I certainly did, you bet," he winked and tapped his nose.

Surprisingly, it was Fred who delivered the killer blow: "even where the sun don't shine?"

Realisation dawned on Maurice and he lifted his head, looking round the group, his face contorted into a grimace; "You bloody sods!"

The laughter was so loud and infectious that everyone around was laughing, even if they didn't know why.

"Can't a man have a little privacy? Need his embarrassments be broadcast to the world? What foul stroke of fate has billeted me with you uncouth Philistines?"

The merriment was infectious and finally, even Maurice laughed at his own misadventure.

24

The air smelt good. The drone of bees and hoverflies carried in the quiet of the morning, butterflies, warmed by the morning sun, fluttered around the herbaceous borders. A few snails, late returning from a night's feasting, left silvery trails as they sought shade beneath the herbage and stones. Overhead, jackdaws circled, back from foraging, throats bulging with food: they landed on the chimney pots where their hungry offspring wrecked the peace with their noisy calls.

Fred stood as usual, savouring the morning solitude. This ritual was born of The Laurels, previously, he never had the aptitude, nor would he spare the time. Looking toward the road, he spotted a stout figure trudging up the drive.

The red pick-up swung through the gateway into the drive, it was driven with reckless haste. It skimmed the pedestrian forcing her to step onto the grass: the pedestrian was Maisie, the cook. The truck screeched to a halt, inches from the front door. The passenger door flew open and Katya jumped out: she never paused, never looked back and kept her head lowered as she passed Fred. She keyed in the door code and entered.

She had exited the truck and disappeared into the house in seconds, but not before Fred had seen the bruised eye and swollen lip. He turned his gaze on the driver: Fred fixed him with a hostile glare, jaw jutting. The pick-up man revelled in it: he thrust his face against the windscreen, lips drawn back in a sneering snarl, teeth white, it was a maniacal face. Fred was incandescent with anger. He felt impotent, helpless. He knew without being told, this was a callous bully: if he had been twenty years younger, he would have dragged him out and given him a pasting.

The sneering lout recognised and revelled in Fred's impotence: he gave him a mocking wave before skidding down the drive. Maisie, walking on the lawn, was showered with gravel. She reached Fred, puffing with exertion and anger, Fred gave her a helping hand up the step. She paused at the door, turning to him.

"Thank you," she set her face with an angry grimace: "if I was feeding that piece of garbage, I'd lace his food with rat poison. I'd watch him squirm and beg and I wouldn't lift a finger to help. Poor Katya: Mavis says she's scared of him but, because she's Polish, won't seek any help. Got no family here, you see. She's a smashing girl: got any ideas?"

Her face softened a little and she smiled at Fred: "How about a nice bread and butter pudding later? I won't put poison in; you look like a man who could do it justice."

Fred gave her one of his rare smiles: "we understand each other."

"We certainly do and if you get a lynching party together, count me in." She gave Fred a poke in the stomach and disappeared into the house.

Fred's morning was spoilt, peace of mind gone, nature's sights and sounds forgotten. He trudged round to Josh's shed.

Josh was pouring the coffee and already had the roll-ups ready. He handed one to Fred and proffered him a light: Fred drew on his cigarette, not speaking. He stared at the ground, brow furrowed.

"Well, something's got your goat."

Fred gulped at his coffee and sucked again on his roll-up. He blew the smoke out slowly and finally looked Josh in the eye.

"Do you ever feel strongly, bloody angry at something and yet feel helpless because you're too weak to do anything about it?" The anger and frustration was plain. It was a new experience for Fred: he had always been in control, confident and able to tackle anything. "Bloody old age!"

They sat awhile, both contemplating. Josh didn't question what the problem could be, but pondered, trying to frame a generalised reply.

"Well, I've had problems like that, when I was growing up. You know the sort of thing, bullying, taunts about your colour by kids who were bigger and tougher. I used to get angry and frustrated. Course, my old man had no time for kid's worries. "Get on with it!"

"My old granddad caught me crying on the way home from school: he coaxed it all out into the open. He was a great man. I told him I was scared of this gang and didn't know what to do. He said don't worry; there's more than one way to skin a cat. Think it through, make your plan and bide your time. Join the boxing club and enlist some help: you can't tackle every problem on your own.

I took up his suggestion and joined a boxing club: I made some good friends. I told the trainer about my problem: he said, you can't beat everybody, but reduce the odds. Two of the older lads were black, like me: I pretended they were my cousins. Between us, we sorted the problem. I had no further trouble. Sometimes you have to seek a bit of help."

Fred sat quietly, pondering; the germ of an idea began to form. His mood lightened, he reached for the birdseed tin: "where's that bloody robin?"

Later, at dinner, the topic of conversation was Katya's black eye: the company were horrified by her injuries. Rose Richardson was seen having a quiet word with her, Katya looked very distressed.

"Why doesn't she go to the police and get something done?" Spike asked.

"It's not that easy for her," Lionel answered, "she's a foreigner in a strange country. She's no family, no friends, except in here: she's afraid of complaining to the police in case it reflects badly on her, worried in case she'd get sent home. She's very good, we need more like her. She's always cheery, never complains and works hard. I'd have her for my daughter anytime. She was an angel to my wife when she was in here."

Fred hadn't realised that Lionel's wife had been a resident. She was at The Laurels for twelve months, very ill. Lionel visited every day to sit with her; he even ate his meals in the home. It was a comfort and sanctuary for him. When she died Lionel, whose son lived in America, entered The Laurel's permanently. He had been resident for several years.

Jane related what she knew of the Katya's unfortunate situation.

"Mavis told me that when Katya first came here and rented her flat, that awful man Craig was working in the adjacent flat. He offered to do a couple of jobs for Katya. He never charged her, they became friendly; she was indebted to him: that's how it began. Now he's turned out to be a controlling monster and she's trapped. I understand Rose tried to intervene and reason with him, but she was threatened and abused. It's terrible."

"Have you seen him? He rolls up to the front door every day at four-o-clock. He sits with his feet on the steering wheel, waiting. He doesn't give a toss about anybody. I wish I could think of something to help," Spike spoke angrily, "there's only one thing that people like him understand and we can't do it."

Fred sat quietly, listening, but passed no comment.

After dinner, there was a buzz around the place: Rose's son Dan was home from college and was going to entertain with his guitar.

"He's very good," Jane was enthusiastic: "he plays and sings beautifully."

"He's marvellous: he lets me play along as the rhythm section," George piped up proudly.

"George loves it," Jane whispered to Fred: "Betty finds him a couple of pans and he drums along. Dan is very good with him: surprisingly, George still has perfect timing, it is good entertainment."

"It would be even better if you still played and joined them," Lionel spoke up.

"No, my playing days are done," Jane replied sadly.

Fred had no great love of music but joined the others. Dan set up in the hall near the piano, most residents sat in the lounge, the double doors open, some sat in the hall. George was positioned by Dan at a small table: Betty produced an upturned jam-kettle and a couple of saucepans. George armed himself with a pair of wooden mixing spoons and a whisk and sat eager, hands poised.

Dan struck up with his guitar, playing and singing some modern classics. Whatever song he played, George automatically picked up the rhythm, varying the volume to suit the song. It was good: Fred, who had no ear for music, was pleasantly surprised. As with all music and especially live entertainment, the residents were rapt, cheering enthusiastically after each number.

Dan was unselfish and chose songs to suit his audience. He played a few country and westerns with a good beat which the crowd loved: the songs also showcased George's talent for drumming. Towards the end of the session, Dan asked if anyone had a request.

"How about 'My Old Man's a Dustman'?" Rita chirped.

Everybody laughed, but Dan obliged, good-naturedly, ripping into it with gusto. As the song reached its final crescendo, George finished with a virtuosic display of drumming to rapturous applause.

"Why don't you put a good word in with your impresario mate," Spike appealed to Maurice: "that lad's talented. Make the effort and give him an opportunity in life, a good deed by you could be life-changing for that boy."

"I can't see Nat Goldman being interested in a lad singing in a care home, even if he is talented," Maurice frowned: "he's got no sentimentality or good-natured attributes; he's only interested in pounds shillings and pence." Maurice held out his hand, rubbing his fingers together: "he's hard as nails."

"Work on him," said Spike: "you can do it, you know him better than anyone."

Maurice looked dubious: he felt Nat Goldman was impervious to any influence he might have.

25

Another day of routines dawned, it was a busy time for the staff; the less able were encouraged and helped from their slumbers and guided and helped through their ablutions. Those that were mobile and able looked after their selves went about their business under the watchful eyes of the staff.

Fred exited the bathroom following his morning ablutions. He was now well used to his incontinence pants: 'piss pants' as he called them.

He had been suffering, unknowingly, from a urinary infection. After it was diagnosed and treated, the major problems eased, but he still dribbled occasionally and continued wearing them. He was comfortable with this, considering how ashamed and embarrassed he had been initially. The main reason for this adaptation was Jane: she had been a rock during this difficult period. Undoubtedly the others had all assisted, but she had taken him under her wing, sharing her own embarrassing affliction with him.

Fred was fond of her, his eyes lit up when she came into the room: they spent many an hour together. They played chess, a game from his childhood which she revived. He never had this closeness with his own wife and he now regretted it: life was too busy, business, business, business. Jane had opened his eyes, helped him see others and the world in a different light. As he would admit, it had come a bit late in life.

As he trundled along the corridor, Cyril emerged from one of the bathrooms. Walking towards them were the 'black widows' and 'Miss Faversham.'

"Good morning, good morning," Cyril greeted the trio of ladies, raising his arm in greeting.

"Ooh! Gracious me! Oh dear! Ladies, about turn! Quickly, don't look!" 'Miss Faversham' hustled her companions in a swift, one hundred and eighty degree turn and backtracked.

Fred could see Cyril was wearing vest and pants. He had hoisted his pants almost to his armpits; the source of the ladies' embarrassment was fully on show. Lionel and Spike emerged from their room to see what the fuss was about.

"Hey up, Cyril, the boys are out of the barracks!" Lionel exclaimed.

Cyril looked bemused. Spike pointed helpfully to the offending area: "down below, Cyril; your tackle's showing."

"Oh dear, oh dear," Cyril shuffled back into the bathroom.

Lionel offered his explanation. "Short underpants and drooping testicles, they just don't go together. I fear the ladies will refuse meat and two veg. for a while."

After breakfast, Rita reported that the Carnival was coming and she was going to see it: she was excited, like a young child.

Spike asked Mary if she liked the carnival and was answered with a raised finger. She watched Spike intently: again, she answered with raised fingers when Spike asked if she liked floats and marching bands. Spike, manoeuvring for a different answer, asked if she liked the dignitaries, the councillors and mayor, this time he was rewarded with a negative finger down.

"Aha! Me also."

Maurice expressed his admiration for Spike "you can't fault him: he's damn good."

Jane explained to Fred that it was an annual event, it passed The Laurels and was good fun: it terminated at the sports ground. Rose and the staff pushed wheelchairs out to the gate and the able-bodied stood and watched. "You might enjoy it, Fred."

"I don't think I'll bother."

"Why ever not?" Spike chided: "it's a spectacle, a change of scene. Sometimes there are a couple of vintage vehicles."

Fred pricked his ears up at this, but didn't commit.

Eleven - thirty, wheelchairs were crunching up the drive: Josh had been recruited to help. The able bodied were making their way with their walking aids. Even Maisie and Betty left the kitchen for a while, shepherding the slow-movers along the drive.

Fred had condescended to go and was leaning on the wall outside The Laurels: across the road were a group of residents from the close opposite. Children were standing, holding bunting and flags: they were excited, jumping up and down, watching for signs of the procession; many were clutching coins in their hand ready to drop in collectors' buckets.

It took Fred back to his childhood, when local carnivals were great entertainment. Fred supposed people weren't so impressed these days, nevertheless, the distant sound of drums caused people to lean forward, straining their necks in an effort to spot the procession.

Fred thought of the ingenuity that went into the creations years ago: people had no money, but would decorate old bikes with homemade coloured paper chains. Paper hats were worn and old clothes with coloured paper pinned to them. Men would black their faces and wear what they thought were cannibals' clothes. They carried homemade spears and terrorized women and children. Some were dressed as Red Indians, whooping and hollering. A couple of horse and carts would be decorated and perhaps a motor lorry carrying the carnival queen. There were always a couple of men dressed as women.

Fred smiled to himself: a lot of it would cause offence these days and be deemed politically incorrect, but it was done with innocence those days, no malice or offence was intended.

The sound of marching bands grew closer: two police motorbike outriders slowly passed, blue lights flashing. They were followed by the first of the marching bands, smart red uniforms, drums and brass instruments: George was beside himself with excitement marching on the spot and beating imaginary drums.

Fred thought back to the simple kazoos and even combs and paper that were used: simple times, simple pleasures. Everyone knew each other those days: there would be banter between the participants and crowd; kids would run alongside, following from start to finish. Sometimes, apples, windfalls, would be thrown from a float to the kids: they would be seized and chomped with relish. No exotic fruits those days.

A couple of small floats followed, groups on the back promoting local charities, round table and the like. Walking groups came after, rattling their buckets at the crowd. A man mounted on a mock-up of an ostrich scampered along the road, he ran across the road to where children stood: they screamed and hid behind their parents. Adults were equally apprehensive, nervous of where the ostrich might poke his beak, many of the women squealed with mock fear.

Across the road, The Laurels' group were delighted with the goings on: Rita was hooting with laughter. The ostrich suddenly made a beeline for the 'black widows' and scampered across the road sideways, the man 'riding' the ostrich put on a show, pretending he had lost control and tugging on the harness. 'Miss Faversham', frowning fiercely, raised her walking stick threateningly; the ostrich adopted a frightened posture and backed away. As 'Miss Faversham' turned back to her companions, the ostrich suddenly launched itself forward thrusting its beak at 'Miss Faversham's' rear. There was great hilarity, Rita was cackling with glee, Maurice chortled at the indignity suffered by 'Miss Faversham'; he well remembered the scolding she had given him. She turned back, face red, stick raised: too late, the ostrich scampered down the road to much cheering.

Following this, a sea- scout band passed by with bugles and drums. Spike shouted across to Fred. "Hey Fred, isn't this one of yours?"

Fred squinted down the road past the marching band: coming towards them was a large, curtain-sided truck; it looked massive, pulled by its tractor unit. The sides were open and decorations could be seen, even from a distance. The livery was immaculate and shone in the sunshine: it was painted in a rich green and red and the lined-out gold writing announced - *'Fred Cox Transport'*.

Fred's mouth dropped open: "what the bloody hell...?"

Fred couldn't bear time-wasting, money-wasting diversions, business was business. Trucks were for the road, earning their keep, not farting about at carnivals.

The tractor unit crept closer, the twin chrome air horns on its roof gleamed, as did the twin stainless exhaust stacks rising vertically at the sides of the cab. It had L.E.D. lighting inside the cab, under Lawrence's supervision, drivers were allowed to customise the interiors somewhat, definitely not allowed under Fred's watch. Lol thought this encouraged pride and 'ownership' amongst the men, he had been proven right: the trucks were kept pristine and scrapes and scratches were minimal.

The truck drew closer, its twin air horns fanfared its arrival. Fred was scowling when the driver and his mate spotted him: "bloody hell, it's Lord Fred!"

They became apprehensive and the air horns were silenced, at that moment heads peeped from the side of the massive trailer. One of them was a girl with long black hair: it was

Fred's Brownie. She spotted Fred and waved vigorously at him, then turned to her friends and pointed to him, they all began waving wildly, peering round the side of the trailer

Fred was nonplussed, wrong-footed. He could see the trailer had been decorated and festooned with garlands and flowers: a large placard read '5th Brownies.'

'Fred's girl' shouted, "Hello, Mr. Frederick!".

Fred slowly raised his walking stick in salute, a grin spread across his face.

The driver and mate were pleasantly relieved and held up their hands in greeting, Fred acknowledged them with his stick and the air horns blasted out a salute.

The rig gleamed, paintwork pristine, it was impressive: Fred was secretly proud. He was also touched by the Brownies' greeting.

As the trailer passed, Fred had a further shock: dressed in uniform assisting 'Brown Owl' and fussing over the girls was a familiar figure - Mercedes.

She waved to him; her face was smiling, bright with pleasure.

Fred didn't know how, or why, but he was pleased, perhaps she had found an interest, something that involved her with children: perhaps it could be making up for her own disappointments. He wondered how she had borne the sadness for all those years, she had never told him, he had never noticed: that typified him.

"Good for her," he thought.

The Rig slowly passed by, Fred watched it go, it was followed by a couple of vintage cars, an ambulance and a fire engine with flashing blue lights: Fred was interested, but his highlight had already passed.

As the residents made their way back up the drive, Spike wheeled his chair side by side with Mary, who was pushed by Josh.

"Wasn't that good Mary?"

Mary raised her fingers.

Noticing this, Josh added, "Did you like the Brownie float?"

Mary raised her fingers.

Behind, the widows were chuntering: "that bird was a disgrace, should have been in the police car."

Behind them, Jane and Fred linked their free arms: Fred's usual frown had vanished and there was a hint of a smile.

Rita shouted after them: "less of that! I'll tell Mrs Richardson!"

26

Fred and Josh sipped and relished their flask coffee: for Fred, it was shared bliss, carved in stone, their routine. The taint of the flask added a distinct flavour, but whether it was their surroundings, or the quiet of the morning, it was heavenly.

The robin was at Fred's feet pecking seed, not yet confident enough to take it from his hand. Suddenly without warning the robin, with a whirr of wings, flew into a thorny shrub against the boundary wall, it tutted angrily. In the quiet of the morning it was startling: Fred and Josh turned to see what had spooked the bird. A flash of slate grey skimmed past Fred's legs and hurtled round the corner of the house; Fred felt the wind from the bird's powerful flight. A bird clucked out a noisy warning, it turned into a pitiful squeak, and then silence.

"It's got him!" Josh exclaimed.

"What the hell was it?" Fred enquired.

"Sparrowhawk, they're deadly. They fly fast and low, ambushing birds, they've got talons like needles. They stretch out their legs and then curtains, kaput, game over. I'll tell you now, Robin had a close shave there; you can see why he's cautious, one eye on the seed and one eye on the look-out.

Fred had never witnessed the like before and was both startled and impressed.

"He comes round often," Josh explained, "he's got a regular route: fortunately, Robin's aware of it, but poor old blackbird wasn't. It's a fickle world, Fred, one minute you're fine, next it's all over."

"Bloody hell; cheer me up, why don't you!"

Josh laughed: "luckily, Fred, we don't generally get razor sharp talons skewering the life out of us." He lapsed into silence, he looked concerned, Fred thought, unusual for Josh.

"Trouble?" Fred enquired.

There was a long pause while Josh framed his reply. "Well, the usual family things," Josh frowned. "You see, my eldest, he's a bright boy, he's at college doing an engineering course, no worries there. But the youngest... well, he's not so bright: good boy mind, but I worry that he could be drifting into bad company. He's not academic and needs something to focus on. The tragedy is, Fred, he's a cracking footballer." Josh shrugged his shoulders.

"If the lad's talented, surely somebody'll spot him," Fred commented.

"His sports master has tried: he asked local clubs to trial him, but no use, no response."

"Ah, but is he that good, or is it just a proud dad's opinion?" Fred raised his eyebrows quizzically.

"He is good Fred and that's not just me saying so. Mr Hendy, the sport teacher says he should be trialling."

"If he's good enough, he'll succeed," Fred assured.

"Yes, but life's not always like that, sometimes you need that bit of luck, that helping hand."

Fred didn't believe in luck, but said nothing: masked by his silence, his mind was working. He stared at the wall as he sucked the dying embers of his roll-up.

Later, at breakfast, Lionel was watching Katya feeding Mary. She was carefully and gently spooning porridge into Mary's mouth encouraging and reassuring her.

Lionel whispered his concerns about Katya: "that girl's had the zest knocked out of her, she seems withdrawn, beaten down: I could weep for her. She was full of life, bubbly, outgoing, now she's quiet: I worry what will become of her. That thug will be waiting at the front door at four-o-clock: it makes my blood boil. Something bad's going to happen to her, I know it."

The group were silent, a sense of gloom prevailed. Fred enquired if he was there every day.

Spike's anger spilled over. "He is, brazen as you like, Mr big bully: feet up on the dashboard as if he owns the place and Katya. If she won't make a complaint though, there's nothing to be done, we're useless."

"Something might turn up," Fred commented.

"I thought you didn't believe in luck," Spike chirped.

"I don't," said Fred with a smile.

After breakfast, Father Murphy the Catholic priest popped in. He moved amongst the residents with a quiet ease, he was the polar opposite to the Rev. Tom, quiet and discreet, but his quiet charm and twinkling smile were equally effective. Fred could see that he was well received: he was welcomed by Catholic and non-Catholics alike. He moved around the lounge sitting and chatting, he obviously brought comfort to people.

"Seems ok," Fred commented to Lionel.

"He is ok, does a good job. It's very comforting if you're a believer, unfortunately, I'm not. I sometimes wish I were: it can ease your mind."

"What do you think, then, about death I mean," Fred felt awkward. The only person he'd discussed the issue with was Josh.

Lionel leant back in his chair looking at Fred. As a retired lecturer, Lionel's opinions were respected by Fred: of course, in Fred's opinion, intellectuals could spout, but couldn't run business, nevertheless...

"For me, Fred, there's no salvation, no paradise, no returning as the angel Gabriel: when you die, that's it."

"There's not much comfort in that," Fred frowned.

"Well, look, I'm not that brave, I cling to the science. Matter and energy never die, they may change their state; they may form new elements and float off into the atmosphere: they could form new life. So, for me, Fred, it doesn't matter if I'm buried, burnt or thrown on the dung heap, I hope to live on in some form. Parts of me may form new life, fly into space, form stars and planets. The way I think, the universe and everything in it is interconnected, of course, it's more comforting if you believe in a God or a creator. I like to think I could be part of a babbling brook, crashing waves, a shooting star even, how about a butterfly, bird, wind and rain? What joy to be forming new life and growth: that'll do for me. Of course, I may be completely wrong and if so, it's eternal damnation, Fred. What do you think Father?"

Father Murphy was passing by but paused and sat in a chair by Fred and Lionel.

"I was just saying, Father, I'm a non-believer, but if I'm wrong I'll probably be cast into the fires of hell."

Father Murphy nodded, "of course you may be right, but I prefer to think that the Almighty would look kindly on a lost soul."

The Father had a quiet wit and humour which Fred found surprising and pleasing. He contrasted it to the clergy of yesteryear with their unforgiving stance, rigid mantras and fearsome presence.

"I believe, if you followed the wrong path but lived a good life based on good deeds, then the good Lord may take a compassionate and forgiving stance. Of course, you'd be hedging your bets," he smiled with a mischievous twinkle in his eye.

Lionel and Fred were of the same mind: this was a clergyman they could respect.

The priest rose from his seat: "gentlemen, if I can be of assistance in any way, don't hesitate to ask."

"Make them do penance, Father, three hail Marys." Rita shouted from the back of the room.

"If they sin too badly, I will." Father Murphy waved to Rita as he made for the door.

"There you go Fred, Father Murphy and the Rev. Tom, both good men: you've got two good examples there, if you feel like following their path."

"Hmm, they're decent blokes," Fred said thoughtfully.

At dinner, Maurice was missing.

"I've heard his cancer's returned, "Lionel whispered; "he doesn't look well lately."

"Brimstone and treacle, that's what he needs," George chirped up: "I had it, sometimes goose grease rubbed on your belly, that does the trick and syrup of figs to keep your bowels free. Yes, that was the stuff, puts you right."

"Yes, but you went to school with Oliver Twist," Spike teased, "treatment's changed a bit now."

"Oliver Twist? I don't remember him, I remember Oliver Arnold; he had warts. My mother rubbed bacon on them and buried it in the garden, it did the trick."

"Your mother must have been the last woman burnt at the stake," Spike grinned.

"Steak? We never had steak. Bread and jam, homemade, mostly damson, she always left the stones in".

"No wonder you've got no teeth," Spike quipped, "and feathers growing on your belly."

After dinner, there was a bingo session, it was well liked: most of the residents indulged. Fred and Lionel never played but watched the proceedings from the side. Lionel was amused by the bingo caller, an elderly gentleman: he would regularly mix up his rhyming ditties, whether purposely or not, no one was sure.

He would call out: "two fat ladies, sixty-six," or "Forty-four, key to the door." This caused hilarity and Rita would shout out: "Silly old fart, that's wrong!"

This session, Fred was absent: he spent the afternoon in his room, with his mobile phone. Mobiles were not commonly used in the home, only one or two residents had them. It was requested they be used only in private rooms, so as not to cause disturbance or disruption. Fred had rarely used his since arriving at The Laurels; he had never been a mobile phone man. Today, though, he had business. He fiddled with a small pocketbook containing numbers.

He laboriously tapped in a number and sat back in his chair, phone to ear.

"Is that you, Garvey?" As usual Fred assumed everyone knew who he was without introduction. His phone manner was gruff and loud, whispering wasn't one of Fred's attributes.

"Look, I need you to get off your arse and do me a favour. Send your scout down to a kid's football match on Saturday morning. Look, don't bloody moan, I'm telling you the kid's good, it's in your interest. Somebody else'll snap him up.

Anyway, I'm sponsoring your bloody kit. Yes, he's a little black kid. Speak to the sports master. Got it?"

Fred concluded the conversation and sat back pondering: "now for the tricky bit." Again, he thumbed through his book and again carefully tapped in the number with his stubby finger.

"Is that you, Bartlett? I've got a cushy number for you. No, I'm not dead yet. No, it's not a bloody breakdown, but you'll need your truck. No, it's not a bloody bank job, shut up and listen; you'll need that big bugger Tadge with you. I'll pay your fee plus a quarter; it's easy money."

Fred was huddled over his phone in detailed discussion for nearly half an hour.

"Well, if you can only manage Saturday it'll have to do. Bloody hell, go on then, fee and a half, Christ, just for a bit of acting, it's a piece of cake. Yes, Saturday at quarter past four. Yes, now sod off."

Fred sat back, a look of satisfaction on his face. It was nearly teatime and he felt peckish. It felt good to be doing something: he was back in harness, useful.

27

It was a takeaway night: everybody was tucking in to their favourite dish. In general, it was welcome and accepted as a rare treat, an air of anticipation pervading the dining room before its arrival. The assembled group had already begun their feast before Maurice appeared late in the dining room, he seemed withdrawn and looked pale.

"Hey Maurice, come on, get stuck in," Spike chivvied.

Maurice remained quiet: he picked over his food, eventually pushing his plate away. He gazed round the room at what he perceived to be a pitiful collection of humanity. Without his own little group, he thought and Spike, in particular, there'd be little conversation or stimulation. It depressed him, lives without meaning or hope. He wondered if dementia sufferers felt this or were they oblivious to it: if Spike and the staff didn't make the effort, communication, for them, would be minimal. How would he cope in those circumstances? His own situation returned to his thoughts, he couldn't bear the thought of infirmity, suffering and slow decline. He had observed first-hand the indignities suffered by those afflicted, the incontinence, the inability to wash or shower, worst of all, inability to feed and the dreadful dribbling. Those thoughts crowded out all others.

He shuddered and turned back to his companions. He looked round at them, good friends; he paused as if gathering himself. Suddenly, he leaned forward and a torrent of words burst from him, his voice forced and strained: "I must tell you, I've had some tests, there's absolutely nothing they can do for me: I'm going to snuff it, the end, kaput."

There was shocked silence.

"The big 'C's returned: the prognosis is terminal, pancreatic cancer. They've given me months, weeks even, I'm scared shitless. I've been plucking up courage to tell you and now I have." He slumped back in his chair, he was drained.

Everyone was shocked, no one spoke for a while; then all chipped in offering sympathy, support and making suggestions.

"Come on, Maurice, surely things can be done?"

"What about 'Chemo'? There's got to be treatment."

"You mustn't give up."

"We're all with you, we'll help you through it, there are new treatments being tried all the while."

Maurice held up his hand. "Not having any, too much pain, lose all my hair. Connected to machines and tubes? No, I'm too big a coward: before it gets too bad, I shall just lie down and die."

"You can't do that!" Spike exclaimed. "You can't just give up and die."

"I will and that's it."

Jane leant across the table visibly upset; she placed her hand over his.

"It's alright, Jane, I've made up my mind. I'd like to say, you have all been good friends: I've led a bit of a selfish life, now I wish I could turn the clock back, but you never can."

Maurice become emotional, he stood, held up his hand and walked from the table.

Jane stood to go after him but Fred, who had said nothing, held her back. "Let him go, best on his own for a while."

George spoke up, "he just needs a good tonic."

"I think he needs a bit more than that George," Lionel responded.

Rose Richardson was talking to Mavis: she watched Maurice leave the table. After her chat, she walked over and sat in Maurice's vacant chair.

"I suppose he's told you, it's so sad. About a year ago he had a section of stomach removed and the signs were hopeful, but now..." Rose shrugged her shoulders: "you know he wants no treatment. We can't do much except be there for him: I know you'll do your bit." She said no more and left the room.

"He's not a bad chap," Lionel remarked sadly: "he says he's had a selfish life and that's probably true. He's vain and a ladies' man but he wouldn't do anybody any serious harm, he wouldn't pass you by if you were in trouble. He's got nobody, nothing. He worked for that impresario fellow for years, got him out of many a scrape, smoothed the way with clients and charmed the women. Nat Goldman had the push and business acumen but was rough and ready: he relied on Maurice, you know. As you would say Fred, he's a bullshitter, but he's harmless really."

Conversation was muted. Generally, after the takeaway and a bottle of beer, tongues would loosen, tonight, however, spirits were low.

Maisie, one of the cooks, was leaving. She had just opened the front door when a demented lady, Elizabeth, threw a tantrum in the hall. Maisie turned back to help Katya, who struggled to calm and control her: Elizabeth was beating Katya with both hands, distressed and in panic. Maisie pinioned Elizabeth's arms while Katya soothed her. Eventually she quietened and they escorted her across the hall, Katya had a scratch mark down her cheek, but was speaking kindly to Elizabeth, stroking her arm.

Just at that moment, Albert, noticing the open front door, made a break for freedom. Considering his age and infirmity, he was out the door like a shot and heading down the drive towards the road.

Everybody was watching the previous incident, George, however, had been sitting in the conservatory and spotted Albert bustling toward the road. He shuffled out into the hall shouting, "Albert's off! He's gone, he's run away!"

Rose Richardson had just descended the stairs into the hallway, having heard the commotion with Elizabeth: she saw George pointing to the open front door and spotted Albert nearing the end of the drive. She kicked off her shoes, hoisted up her skirt and sprinted along the gravel drive. She reached him and grabbed his arm as he exited the gateway. She slowly trudged back with a sheepish Albert: as she entered the front door she was gently chiding him.

"Albert, I don't want a hundred-yard sprint at this time of day, nor my time of life. Where were you going?"

"Late for work! Late for work!" he protested.

"I tell you what; have a day off, you deserve it."

She shut the front door as Maisie rushed up, red faced and breathless.

"I'm so sorry, Mrs Richardson. I left the door open."

"It's ok Maisie, I saw what happened: you'd got your hands full. You get off home and thanks for your help. Don't worry about it."

Jane and Fred stood in the hall as Rose passed leading Albert towards the lounge: she gave them a grim smile.

"You're only a hair's breadth away from disaster in this job: if you let your guard down, for an instant, you are in trouble." She gave a sigh and a weary smile: "and poor Katya, another mark on her face, what's to be done for that girl?

28

Fred was up early: it was Saturday morning and he was looking forward to his 'roll-up', not only that, he also had a muted sense of elation and a controlled sense of pleasant anticipation.

Josh had shown Fred where the shed key was hidden, under a stone. He also left him two cigarettes in a jar, on a shelf, with a warning: "one for Saturday, one for Sunday. If you smoke both on Saturday, that's your lot."

He stood waiting outside the front door: he was gasping for a smoke but he waited. The morning was dull with a slight breeze, although the day was mild, Fred shivered slightly: he shuffled his feet to keep his circulation.

Betty, one of the cooks, strolled up to the door and keyed in the security number, she gave Fred a nod and asked, in her blunt fashion, what he was hanging about for.

Fred tapped his nose: "business."

"Oh," Betty nodded her head vigorously and went in.

The red truck roared up the drive and skidded to a halt close to the front door: the driver smirked at Fred, pulled Katya over and forced a kiss on her lips. He never once took his eyes off Fred and when Katya pulled herself away, he still smirked.

Katya was pale, the once cheeky face, grim: her spark had gone. She passed Fred with a nod and a weak smile, the scratch on her face stood out vividly against her sallow features.

Fred, usually simmering with rage, would normally have given Craig his best scowl. This morning though, he was calm, he grinned at the thug.

Craig sneered, but was unsettled by Fred's unusual demeanour. He gesticulated with his middle finger: Fred merely broadened his grin, showing his teeth, as the truck skidded up the drive.

Fred stood for a few minutes then marched round the side of the house, swinging his walking stick. The effort cost him dear and when he reached Josh's shed he was coughing and gasping for breath. When the coughing fit eased, Fred retrieved the key from under the stone and unlocked the shed. He pulled out the old tatty chair and lit up his cigarette. He was calm, at ease, and drew in his first fix of nicotine, leaning back in the chair. The robin appeared: it perched on a garden stake and watched Fred keenly. It cocked its head on one side, its bright eyes fixed on Fred who got up quietly, went in the shed, and retrieved the seed tin. He sprinkled a few grains onto the ground in front of the chair and waited.

The robin, after a pause, flew down and pecked eagerly at the seed: its eyes flicking between Fred and the seed. Fred waited and watched as the bird pecked the last of the seed. It cocked its head in anticipation of more reward, Fred waited, sitting still: the bird flew back onto the stake.

"It's not that easy: if you want some more you've got to earn it. Give me a bit of trust."

Fred tipped a few grains into the palm of his hand. He rested his arm on the chair with hand open. Minutes passed by, Fred watched the robin and the robin watched Fred. All the time the bird cocked its head from one side to the other, assessing Fred: the food was there, but what was the risk? Could it be a trap?

Suddenly, the bird darted at Fred's hand, barely landing and snatched a grain of seed. It flew straight back to the stake, swallowed the seed and watched Fred for a reaction.

Fred didn't move, he sat motionless; he never even puffed on his cigarette: he felt a rising sense of anticipation and had to hold himself in check.

The bird, after cocking its head, flew off the perch and landed on Fred's stubby thumb: it paused, again watching Fred. With one eye on the food and one on Fred, it hopped into the palm of his hand, grabbed food and hopped back onto his thumb.

Fred was mesmerised. He hardly dared breathe, but he knew he'd won the bird over: he'd done it. He'd rarely felt such a sense of achievement. For the next few minutes, the robin hopped from thumb to palm, grabbing food, each time it watched Fred, assessing him, finally trusting him.

Fred was convinced the robin was smiling. Its bright twinkling eyes bewitched him and he couldn't stop the flush of pleasure and the grin that crept across his face. Nobody would have believed Fred Cox had been enchanted by a small bird, let alone have the patience to do it.

"You know, Robin, between you and me, I've got a feeling it's going to be a good day today: a bloody good day."

29

Maurice was missing at breakfast. At dinner, he appeared, sat at the table and looked round with a faint, resigned smile. He looked calm, as if he had come to terms with his prognosis: he spoke quietly and politely to his companions. There was relief: they had feared the first contact following the shocking news. No one, not even Jane could bring themselves to ask how he was, it was left to Spike to break the ice. His enquiry was casual, a nonchalant "how are you doing?"

Maurice responded calmly: "Not bad at all, I'm fine."

The relief was palpable and the mood lifted, normal banter resumed. George drummed on the table telling everyone Maurice had taken a tonic: Maurice smiled when George vowed "you'll be alright now."

Spike made a suggestion: "I've got a drop of sherry, why don't we have a little tipple tonight? Perk us up."

Lionel agreed; he could rustle up half a bottle of port: Fred didn't drink, but was assured it wasn't strong stuff, more like pop. Maurice seemed pleased with the idea, so they agreed to meet after evening beverage in Spike and Lionel's room. Jane declined, reluctantly: it was a man's gathering. It would be good for Maurice.

Dinner passed convivially. There was an uncomfortable moment when the widows asked Katya about her scratched face: "did that oafish man of yours cause that?" One asked belligerently.

"No, not this time," Katya answered quietly.

"I should hope not: he needs to feel the full force of the law. You deserve much better my dear." She patted Katya's hand kindly.

Katya was touched by her kindness and thanked her, she was tearful.

Lionel yearned for justice and retribution, he was angry and frustrated. The others were of the same mind: there was wild talk of ganging up on Craig, make some cudgels, beat him to pulp. Someone volunteered Maisie and Betty, they'd sort him, batter him to death with their rock cakes.

"Grab him by the balls!" Rita shouted from the back. She had no idea what they were talking about but it lightened the mood. Sadly, the problem remained unresolved.

Fred remained quiet.

Saturday afternoon saw an increase in visitors: those without, generally napped. Fred had received a visit from Mercedes and Lol on Thursday, so avoided the lounge. Jane was chatting to Maurice in the veranda. Fred wandered through the hall, passing Rose Richardson's office, the door was open and Rose was gazing out of the window.

"A penny for them!"

"Oh hello, Fred, come in. I was just daydreaming, you know what it's like; you're never free of worries." She smiled at Fred offering him one of her mints. "Daughter finishing her social study degree, very capable: love to have her here, but without some investment, can't do it."

"There's always a solution."

"Well maybe there is, Fred. I just can't see it at the moment, but never mind, we keep plodding on. How are you doing?"

"I'm fairly good at the moment, but I've got a little bit of business coming up and I may need your help; in strictest confidence of course."

"Of course, Fred: how can I help?"

At tea, Fred was clock-watching throughout, causing Spike to ask if he had a date lined up.

At four-o-clock the red truck screeched to a stop outside the front door, so close that a couple of elderly visitors had to squeeze past. The elderly lady stumbled and almost fell: her companion looked indignantly into the truck where the driver lounged, feet up on the steering wheel. Craig had his hands clasped behind his head; he grinned at their discomfort and turned his music up to a loud volume.

In the dining room the bass beat of the music could be felt through the Georgian walls, Katya quietly went about her business ferrying residents to the toilet and helping to spoon-feed the less able. She never looked up when the loud music boomed out, she looked uncomfortable but kept her head down.

"It's that twisted psychopath, he loves bullying and terrorising people," Lionel spoke angrily. Generally a mild man, it was rare to hear his voice raised.

The front end of the red pick-up was visible from the dining room and the diners were used to its arrival. Everyone turned and looked towards the source of the sound: Craig grinned at the turned faces and turned the volume up even higher.

"That's not music, it's just a row," George complained.

"It's Katya's chap," Rita piped up, "he's an arse!"

Anybody looking out of the windows, at quarter past four, would have seen a huge shape filling The Laurels' gateway. It was a four-axle, heavy breakdown truck of massive proportions, it barely squeezed past the brick pillars. The height of the cab hardly fitted under the tree canopy that overhung the drive. It had a gleaming row of large chrome headlights on the cab roof; the paintwork was royal blue and white. The red nomenclature on the sides and cab front read *'Bartlett, Heavy Recovery Specialist.'*

The colossus crept slowly up the drive, its huge engine barely ticking over. In deference to the residents, it proceeded steadily, only the crunch of gravel beneath the chromed wheels indicated its presence: that and the shadow it cast over the dining room windows.

In the dining room, heads turned: many residents stood and looked out of the windows. Fred got to his feet and hurried into the veranda for a better view: he was followed by others.

"What the hell's that thing doing up here?" Spike asked incredulously, wheeling his chair into the veranda.

"Could be some entertainment here;" Fred was grinning.

Spike looked suspiciously at him, but said nothing.

As the truck crept alongside the veranda, the array of headlamps on the roof illuminated, giving off a dazzling white light. Rita, with others, was transfixed by the spectacle, she gave out a whoop. In the cab behind the driver and the passenger was an array of fairy lights spelling out 'Tadge and Geoff, Road Kings', on the radiator grill was a plaque with 'Dreadnought' inscribed.

Geoff Bartlett was old school, like Fred. He was in his late sixties, stocky with huge forearms. He had far more humour than Fred, though, and indulged his young protégé, allowing him to decorate the cab. Geoff had no children of his own: he had given the young Polish man, Tadeusz, a job and, five years on, Tadge was like a son to him. Geoff admired his hard work, strength and above all, his steadfast, good-natured character. They had clicked, immediately, and there was a bond of mutual trust between them.

The truck advanced slowly towards Craig's red pick-up. The driver, Tadge, gave the residents a wave and a friendly grin: he held his hand up in a regal wave. Rita was ecstatic and waved excitedly. Craig had now taken his feet off the steering wheel; he was scowling at the approaching mass. The truck closed in on the pick-up: both driver and mate were grinning down at Craig. The truck inched inexorably towards the pick-up, dwarfing it: Craig was now anxious and a look of panic replaced his usual cocky sneer.

"Crush him, crush him!" Rita shouted.

Those manning the windows in The Laurels held their breath in anticipation. At the last second, the loud hiss of the air brakes halted the truck, a hair's breadth from the pick-up. The engine stopped with a shudder and the 'monster' stood quieted.

Craig, the thug, suddenly came to life. The fear had now turned to anger and he sprang out of the pick-up, face contorted. He strode to the front of the truck, white faced and inspected the pick-up's bumper and the massive towing hitch of the recovery rig. His lips formed an angry scowl and he glared up at the truck's cab.

The recovery truck's driver flung open the cab door. The driver's seating position was elevated, but Tadge hopped nimbly to the ground, again waving to the faces at the windows: the watchers missed nothing. His toothy grin never left his face; he was swarthy with dark eyes and dark thick hair. He was well over six feet in height, broad and well built. With long strides, he rounded the front of the truck and grinned at the pick-up driver: Craig stood on the other side. He looked down at the bumpers and then aggressively at the stranger: he shouted an angry challenge to Tadge, pointing to his bumper.

The grin never left Tadge's face. He jumped onto the bumper of the red truck and stepped across between the vehicles, his bulk caused the pick-up's nose to dip.

Craig stood, legs akimbo, pointing angrily to the bumper: the stranger was now facing Craig and for the first time Craig realised he was dealing with a large, formidable figure. Tadge bent slightly and placed his hand under the bumpers, indicating that there was daylight between. He stood grinning.

"Nice truck man, I wouldn't scratch that." He tapped Craig's cheek in a mock-friendly fashion, but with enough force to make the thug blink.

"Very nice, very smart: you look after it now," he poked Craig in the chest with his fore finger. Leaning forward, he looked into Craig's eyes and gave him a last grin before hopping back on the bumper.

In the house Rita was shouting: "Hit him, hit him!" Everybody was willing it to happen, even the widows pressed their noses to the window hoping for retribution on Craig.

Craig stared uneasily after the big man, he watched him approach the front door of The Laurels: his size, his fearlessness and also the hint of a foreign accent unsettled him.

The passenger door of the recovery truck opened and a burly, thick-set, man lowered himself steadily to the ground: Geoff Bartlett grinned at Craig. He was short and barrel-chested, with faded tattoos on his thick forearms.

"Nice SUV:" he studied Craig's truck, kicking its tyres with his greasy boots, "does it do any work?"

Katya's boyfriend had lost his bluster and merely shook his head, asking anxiously: "here for a job?"

Geoff adopted a serious face, pursing his lips: "no, Tadeusz has come to see his cousin; he hasn't seen her for a couple of years. Polish, like him, you know."

Craig became agitated: "do they keep in touch?"

Geoff shook his head: "not for a while, but I believe she's got boyfriend troubles. Shacked up with some bastard by all accounts: no problem though, Tadge'll sort things.

The thug's shifty eyes watched the front door: bravado had turned to nervous apprehension.

30

Rose Richardson opened the front door and welcomed Tadge to The Laurels: "come and have a coffee with us."

Tadge shook her hand and gave a little bow, Rose was charmed. She guided him to a chair in the hallway and ordered a coffee from the kitchen: she told them he was Katya's cousin and had come to visit. Rose gave Tadge a wink and left to brief Katya.

Maisie and Betty both left the kitchen to serve Tadeusz with coffee and cake: they were immediately taken with him, impressed with his manners and physique.

"Hope you might be able to help Katya with a few problems she's having," Betty said with a meaningful glance at Maisie.

"Don't worry, ladies, things will be fine, no troubles." Tadge smiled exuding an air of total confidence.

The cooks were charmed: could there be a change of fortune for Katya? They hoped.

Rose called Katya out of the dining room and with her arm round her shoulders, explained that she had a visitor, a cousin. She would probably not recognise him but, even so, welcome him as if you know him, a long lost relative.

"It could have a good outcome, Katya, trust me: play along with it."

Rose spoke earnestly and Katya, although confused, had confidence in her. She had a sense of anticipation, but who was this man and what was he doing here?

Katya followed Rose into the hall: as she crossed the hall, a smiling bear of a man rose from a chair and greeted her in Polish.

"Czesc Katya." He picked her up and whirled her round planting a kiss on both her cheeks.

Katya was surprised, but in a pleasant way: her cheeks flushed with pleasure. Her 'cousin' lowered her to the floor, his face showed genuine pleasure. He bowed slightly and placed a hand on his heart: "Tadeusz, Tadge," he spoke his name by way of introduction, bowing once again.

Katya was charmed and her face brightened and some of the dullness faded from her eyes: it was the old Katya. Betty and Maisie peered round the kitchen door nudging each other delightedly, was this Katya's knight in shining armour? They hoped so.

Katya looked up at the smiling face. "Hello Tadeusz."

Tadge whirled her round again and they chatted excitedly in Polish.

Outside, Geoff Bartlett was relishing his new role and was speaking with exaggerated nonchalance to Craig. He was well aware of the audience at the windows and had spotted Fred Cox in the veranda. He was determined to put on a good show, he knew Craig was rattled and placing his brawny hand on the red pick-up he leant close to Craig as he spoke.

"You know, he's a gentle giant, is Tadge, but...," he raised a stubby finger and leant towards Craig as if sharing a secret, "if he loses it..." He tapped the side of his head with an oily finger, a grim look on his face.

It was theatrical, designed to entertain the watching audience and intimidate Craig: He continued.

"We were doing a job once; an artic had a burnt out a wheel bearing in a town centre. It was a Saturday afternoon, a gang of tanked-up yobs were jeering at us: it didn't worry us. We just got on with the business. The next thing, they were pushing and goading an old man who was passing. Well, Tadge was straight across to help. The ring leader thought he was Mr Big and pulled a knife on him: was that a mistake?"

He paused for effect, looking over his shoulder as if checking no one was about.

"Next up, Tadge had him by the balls, by the time I pulled him off; the yob was screaming and crying. The rest of his gang fled, pissing their pants."

Again he paused looking over his shoulder; Craig meanwhile was quaking, hanging on to every word, at the same time glancing fearfully at the front door. Geoff Bartlett leant in to Craig, his face up close, again looking over his shoulder, his voice was a whisper.

"They say; one of his balls had burst: it was like spaghetti in his pants." He grimaced horribly: "I doubt whether he'd father any kids after that," he shook his head sadly.

Craig was ashen: the bully was cowed, swagger gone. He moved round to the pick-up's door, eyes on The Laurels' front door.

"You're not going, are you?" Geoff pleaded, "Tadge loves to talk trucks, he'll be out any minute. Is that him?" Geoff looked over his shoulder.

Craig leapt into his red truck and reversed. As he did so, he spotted the old man grinning at him, his face pressed up against the window, "the old bastard!" He shot up the drive and out the gate: cheering broke out from the house, Geoff Bartlett turned, pleased with his efforts and gave a small bow.

Even Fred was impressed and gave him a secret 'thumbs up.' The front door opened and Betty emerged with a mug of tea and a plate of cakes.

"I don't know what you did, you and your mate, but good on yer. We were hoping you were going to give him a good duffing," she spoke with relish. "Any time you're passing here, there'll always be tea and cakes."

"Glad to be of service," Geoff beamed, giving Betty a wink: "no need for violence. A quiet word is all it takes." He swigged his tea and scoffed his cakes chatting happily with Betty.

Katya emerged from the house with Tadeusz, his arm round her shoulders.

"I think we should give this young lady a lift home, Geoff, make sure she's ok."

"If you say so Tadge: I think he's found a soft spot for you, young lady." Geoff was pleased.

"Please Mr Bartlett, call me Katya and thank you so much. I don't understand how this has happened, but thank you, thank you both." Tears welled up in her eyes.

Tadge lifted her up like a doll into the cab. "You've got friends now: everything's alright."

The heavy recovery truck reversed slowly up the drive; the audience at The Laurels' windows were ecstatic: it was the best entertainment they'd had for many a while. As they turned away from the windows there was a general feeling of satisfaction, none more so than with Fred Cox. The house was abuzz with the events, everyone discussing what they had seen.

"What good fortune for Katya. I'm so pleased for her. Fancy, a cousin she hadn't seen for years turning up, just at the right time. What a fortuitous coincidence," Jane said delightedly.

"Rose has had something to do with it, I'll wager," Lionel added.

"Somebody certainly has," Spike was looking hard at Fred.

The evening passed, the conversation still centred round the truck and Craig's come-uppance: it was likely to be a topic for many a while.

At nine-o-clock, Fred, Maurice and George gathered in Spike and Lionel's room. George stayed for five minutes only: nine p.m. was his bedtime. He sipped a small glass of sherry smacking his lips with relish: although not understanding Maurice's illness, he shook his hand vigorously as he left.

"You'll be fine. Just keep taking the tonic."

Maurice smiled and thanked him: George had a good heart, even though rationality was ebbing away from him. Jane had declined the invitation, declaring that it was 'a men's night'. The foursome sipped their sherry and port: the evening's events were still fresh.

"I wish I knew what those truck blokes said to him," Spike grinned, "he couldn't get out of the drive quick enough."

"His face was whiter than a parson's dog collar: do you think he'll be back?" Maurice seemed perky. The excitement of the events and the comforting warmth of a glass of port had lifted his spirits.

Fred sipped his sherry cautiously, he wasn't a drinker, but found it pleasant. "I don't think we'll see that prick again and good riddance to him."

"We'll all drink to that and good luck to Katya too, I think she's clicked with that big bloke, cousin or no cousin." Again, Spike looked suspiciously at Fred.

They clinked glasses, the atmosphere was jovial; they were at ease. After a second glass, they were emboldened, normal reserve faded.

"Now, 'Maureece', what's to be done about you?" Spike asked: "what about your treatment?"

Maurice was calm, mellow but firm. "I've told you chaps, I'm having no treatment, no drugs and no tubes. I've settled my mind to it. In any case, soon, my money runs out, I can't bear sharing a room like you two reprobates. My guts are beginning to rebel at many foods I used to like and my desire for the fairer sex is fading fast. When I feel the time is right, I shall just depart this world: for where I know not. I don't wish to argue with you chaps so I hope you'll respect my wishes."

There was silence for a while: nobody argued with Maurice. They had tried previously; they didn't agree but accepted his wishes. They felt a comradeship, a bond, closeness. Perhaps the drink encouraged it, but that, and their situation in The Laurels, drew them closer together.

To everyone's surprise, Fred, chin jutting, mouth set, reached out his brawny hand: "We're all with you."

The words were short and gruff but Maurice was touched. He reached out his long bony fingers and grasped Fred's hand. Immediately, Lionel slapped his hand on theirs and Spike followed. They grasped hands in silence, they were as one; they could lean on each other. For Fred, a singularly independent man, it was a new experience, forged in the confines of a care home, a setting where people faced their own mortality. Face it alone or together: Fred had joined a club.

Membership might be short.

31

Sunday at The Laurels was routine apart from the usual daily traumas. Fred rose later than usual: last night's reverie with Maurice and the boys, coupled with the alcohol, ensured he slept in. He was too late to sneak round to Josh's shed and thus missed his morning cigarette.

Albert appeared at breakfast, staggering, seemingly dizzy, Lionel and Fred stood to steady him; thinking he was about to collapse. He was trying to explain something, but his muddled burbling made no sense. They helped him to a chair; he continued to burble and protest.

"Teeth, teeth," he repeated pointing at his mouth, "teeth gone." He poked his tongue out to emphasise the point.

Mavis came to assist and looked in his mouth to check if his teeth were in place.

"No, no, teeth, teeth!" he became frustrated: Mavis was baffled. They stood, making suggestions to Albert, trying to hit on the problem, all the while he grew more irritated, frustrated by his inability to explain his dilemma. They were unable to solve the conundrum: they stood round him thwarted, their best efforts had failed.

On the verge of giving up Spike suddenly shouted "Eureka!" Turning from his conversation with Mary, he'd spotted a lens was missing from Albert's spectacles. Mavis found it on the floor in his room. Spike pressed it back into the frame, tightened the retaining screw with the tip of his penknife, behold, equilibrium was restored.

Albert beamed: "I told you teeth, teeth."

"Sorry," Mavis said apologetically, "I should have known!"

"You need a bit more training in gobbledy-gook," Lionel suggested.

Conversation still centred round Geoff Bartlett's recovery truck and yesterday's drama. It dominated the day, it transformed dull routines.

Maurice seemed light-hearted, he was talkative; last night's gathering had been good therapy. They had exorcised previous unspoken and awkward issues, burdens had been shared and lightened; life and death issues had been discussed openly. Everyone present had bonded and departed the better for it, even Fred.

Lawrence and Mercedes popped in after dinner: what was once a chore, was now pleasurable. Fred was talkative, full of humour, the transformation was remarkable. "Who was this man?"

"I hear Geoff Bartlett was up here with his truck, yesterday," Lol commented, "what was that all about? I wouldn't think there'd be any breakdowns here." He grinned and raised his eyebrows.

"Was it something to do with you, Fred?" Mercedes asked.

"Mind your business!" Fred retorted, looking somewhat pleased with himself.

"They tell me you were up late having a drink with the boys," Mercedes remarked mischievously.

"There are too many nosy sods round here: keep this out of it." Fred tapped the end of his nose with his finger.

Cyril appeared and caused much mirth. Here he was, a man of ninety, wearing a black T-shirt: it was emblazoned with lurid red script, 'Black Sabbath'.

Maurice was choking with laughter: "Isn't that one of yours? Cyril certainly looks the business in it."

Spike turned: "Bloody hell, doesn't Maureen ever wear her glasses?"

Maureen was the large and fierce laundry lady. She was renowned for mixing up the laundry, seemingly too proud to wear her glasses.

"They're all labelled properly, that's what annoys me," Spike moaned.

"Tell her, give her a good dressing down, you can't have that. They're clearly labelled," Lionel prodded.

Spike watched the formidable figure pushing her trolley: "no thank you, tomorrow perhaps." He turned back continuing his conversation with Mary. "What did you think of that big truck yesterday?"

Mary raised her finger watching Spike intently.

"Brilliant, wasn't it?" Spike responded: "what about that Craig?"

Mary lowered her finger.

"He certainly got his come-uppance, that's for sure."

Mary raised her finger.

"Do you think there could a bit of romance starting between that Tadge fellow and Katya?" Spike asked.

Mary raised her finger.

"I think so too: I think we'd like that."

Mary raised her finger.

It was one of those contented days at The Laurels when the world didn't seem such a bad place after all.

32

Monday dawned and Fred was up early. He had retired early following the week-end's events, but he woke refreshed, keen and eager to talk with Josh and sample his cigarette. Mandy let him out: it was an open secret that Fred sneaked a fag with Josh, but no-one let on.

Fred stood on the step waiting, slightly anxious. A plump figure appeared at the end of the drive, it was Betty the cook. As she reached Fred she smiled and poked him in the chest.

"You're a dark horse you: I know what you're waiting for."

Fred frowned: "don't know what you're on about."

Betty tapped her nose and entered The Laurels.

A couple of minutes later, a slim figure walked briskly up the drive: Fred squinted at the approaching figure. He visibly relaxed when he recognised Katya. He looked around feigning indifference.

"Czesc, Mr Cox." Katya's mischievous smile lit her face.

"Don't give me that foreign shite," Fred said gruffly.

"I don't know how you did it and I know you'll deny it, but thank you."

She kissed Fred on the cheek and was gone before Fred could respond.

The late summer morning was cool, but Fred was flushed with pleasure. He stepped down onto the path and shuffled briskly round the corner: he could barely wait to get to Josh's shed. He paid for his haste at the back corner of the house when the usual coughing fit caused him to lean on the house wall. He rubbed his chest as a sharp pain assailed him. After a few minutes it subsided and he set off once more with caution. Josh was pulling out the chairs as Fred approached: Fred slumped into his chair.

"Come on get the bloody fags out," he groused.

Josh grinned: "I notice you only smoked one over the weekend. That's a first."

"Too bloody busy," Fred complained, "I'll have two this morning to catch up."

"I don't know whether that's allowed." Josh frowned, pondering.

"Come on, come on; bloody hell!"

Josh grinned, relented and lit the cigarettes. He watched Fred sucking in his nicotine fix. Neither spoke for a few minutes. Fred was agitated and Josh could see he was itching to report his news.

"Come on then. What have you been up to?"

"Me? Nothing much, but we had a good afternoon's entertainment on Saturday."

Normally sparing with his conversation, Fred struggled to maintain his usual reticence.

"That bastard Craig, you know, Katya's chap. Well, he received a bit of come-uppance." Fred paused, keeping himself in check and Josh in suspense.

"A long-lost Polish cousin of Katya's turned up, seeking her out. He and his mate had a quiet word with the thug. Following that, would you believe, Craig left and hasn't been seen since."

"Hmm, Craig seems to have been persuaded easily," Josh puckered his face up in mock surprise.

"Well, the cousin was built like a brick shithouse." Fred paused puffing his cigarette before gleefully announcing: "he disappeared up the drive as if his arse was on fire, he won't come back." The descriptive effort caused Fred another coughing fit and he sat quietly when it subsided.

Josh watched him with a wry smile: "and you had nothing to do with it, eh?

"No, nothing to do with me," Fred asserted. They sat quietly for a while sipping their coffee.

"I've got some good news of my own."

Fred grunted, watching Josh's eager expression.

"A scout from the 'Rovers' turned up to watch my lad's team playing football, can you believe it? He invited my lad to go to a training session at the 'Rovers' for a trial. I tell you what, Fred, I'm over the moon. It could be an opening for him."

"That's a stroke of good luck," Fred spoke softly: "I'm pleased for the lad."

"You told me you didn't believe in luck," Josh retorted, watching Fred out the corner of his eye.

"Well, maybe sometimes it plays a part." Fred looked into the distance avoiding eye contact with Josh. Fred rose to his feet: "it's that bird."

Before Josh could move, Fred reached into the shed for the seed tin. Josh watched quietly. Impatiently, Fred fumbled with the lid but finally had seed in his hand. He threw a little onto the ground and immediately the robin flew down to take the treat. Next, Fred leant back in his chair, poured a little seed into his outstretched hand and waited quietly.

Josh sat still watching Fred's expression. Fred's face was eager with anticipation but quite calm. Minutes passed: the robin was perched on a garden fork turning its head from side to side.

"Not ready yet, Fred." Josh thought to himself.

Suddenly the robin flew directly onto Fred's thumb. It was at ease, its bright eye watching Fred as it pecked the seed from his hand.

Fred was triumphant: he grinned at Josh whilst keeping the rest of his body stock still.

"Well, well, Fred," Josh spoke quietly with a smile, "you're definitely one of us. What do you say, Robin?"

The bird cocked its head on one side as if responding: Fred beamed.

"It's been a bloody good week," he whispered, "light up that other fag and pour me some more coffee."

33

Rain pattered on the front windows: autumn's arrival brought mixed weather, dark nights and early morning frosts. Today, though, was a wet but mild day.

In the afternoon the residents gathered, many in the hall, some in the lounge. The double doors were opened so everyone could see into the hall. Residents from the first-floor nursing section, who were not bed-ridden or too frail, were brought down in the lift. There were a few visitors. It was a musical afternoon: entertainment was generally relished amongst those gathered.

Rose Richardson's son, Dan, was home from college. He sat on a stool in the middle of the hall with his guitar. He sang a selection of folk and traditional tunes, specially chosen to suit his audience, old favourites. His talent shone through, irrespective of the type of music: his voice had range and versatility; he could switch effortlessly between different genres and styles. He threw in a sprinkling of classics, by modern composers. His lyrics were clear, he didn't mumble like many modern musicians. Whether singing softly, or with a raucous edge to his voice, the words were crystal clear. His guitar accompaniment was immaculate and skilled. He was appreciated. His fair hair and delicate features endeared him to his audience: he was an easy-going lad with his mother's characteristic good humour and compassion.

George, the former drummer, was sat at a small table to the side. On the table was a mish-mash of metal pots and pans: he was armed with a pair of drumsticks. Dan always invited George to accompany him; it was the highlight of the week for George. When music struck up, George was transformed, his dementia retreated: his inbuilt sense of rhythm, unaffected by his affliction, surfaced with surprisingly good results. He automatically struck the right rhythm, picked the most suitable utensil, drummed softly or energetically to suit the tune. He would end each tune with a virtuoso flourish but never overpowered Dan. It was a miracle to behold. The audience was appreciative, clapping and cheering as required.

"You know, that lad's talented," Lionel addressed his companions.

"He certainly is," Jane Appleby responded, "he deserves an opportunity to show the world his talent."

"What about that pal of yours, Maurice; that impresario, I thought he was coming to see him play?"

Maurice frowned: "well I did ask him and he said he'd come. He owes me plenty of favours: plenty." He drifted into thought.

"He's just another bullshitter, I suppose," Fred interjected.

Fred had no real appreciation for music but even he recognised Dan's talent.

Dan finished his performance to much applause and generously thanked George for accompanying him. That received a further burst of applause, much to George's delight.

Rose Richardson thanked her son and George and introduced a silver haired, distinguished gentleman from the back of the room. He was dapper, dressed in dark suit and tie.

"Please, everyone a big welcome for Mister Bertrand Fosdyke."

The crowd clapped: Mr Fosdyke had entertained previously and was well received. He was in his eighties but sprightly. He had been a teacher for forty years at a local Grammar School; he taught Geography and had been a leading light in amateur dramatics. He generously visited local hospices, care homes and retirement clubs: he offered his own brand of entertainment for the price of afternoon tea.

He bowed slightly to the audience and sat at the piano. He played a flourishing intro., then turned and recited a monologue, 'Albert and the Lion'. It was an old favourite and went down well with the crowd. He followed this with some Flanders and Swan ditties: accompanying himself at the piano he gave renditions of 'When the Gasman Came to Call' and 'Mud, Mud, Glorious Mud.' His sonorous, theatrical voice and perfect English diction gave humour and respect to the songs. He needed no microphone; he could project his voice to the back of the room effortlessly.

He stood and bowed to the gathering, receiving his applause: "one last request, anyone?"

A raucous voice shouted from the back of the hall: "how about some rock and roll?" It was Rita. "How about 'Rock Around the Clock'?" she persisted.

"Well, I... well, I haven't really got that music," Mr Fosdyke stuttered.

"Come on, you can do it," Rita pleaded.

"Well, if someone's got the music I'll give it a go," Mr Fosdyke said gamely.

Dan, who had been sitting at the side, stood and proffered Mr Fosdyke a battered music book: 'Rock and Roll Classics'.

Mr Fosdyke, a real trouper, thumbed through the book until he found the song.

"Well," he said, "well, let's give it a go, shall we?" He turned from the piano and nodded up to Rita.

"Now for some fun," Spike chortled.

"Oh, it's not fair," Jane pleaded, "it's not his sort of music."

"He's going for it," Lionel said excitedly.

Mr Fosdyke struck up the piano introduction with gusto, bouncing up and down in his seat and then leapt into the vocals with enthusiasm "One two, three-o-clock, four-o-clock rock......."

His perfect, clipped, Oxford English rattled off the lyrics. The piano bounced out the rock and roll rhythm. The contrast was startling, hilarious but entertaining.

Spike was hooting behind his hand and Jane had her handkerchief to her mouth, tears of laughter running down her face. Even Fred, who was tone deaf, was smirking.

The song reached its finale: people were tapping their feet enthusiastically.

Mr Fosdyke played out the finale with vigour, his fingers dramatically punching the piano keys. He finished, stood, turned and threw open his arms to rapturous applause. Rita was clapping and whooping. Mr Fosdyke bowed to her and crossed the floor, a bounce in his step. He made for the kitchen to claim his cream tea and sandwiches.

"You know, I may just add that to my repertoire," he beamed to Rose Richardson.

34

Autumn's mellowness continued through late October. Clocks were set back to Greenwich Mean Time: days shortened and nights drew in.

It was an uneventful day, although an outsider might have disagreed. Petty calamities and minor disasters were part and parcel of a normal day at The Laurels.

A small highlight for residents was the arrival at the front door of Tadge, Katya's new man. The blossoming romance was cause for delight and to the residents it certainly looked to be a match made in heaven. The contrast between Tadge and 'the thug' was remarkable: Tadge was ever amiable and cheery. He drove up to the front door in a battered old van, he waved and smiled to whoever peered out of the windows and blew kisses to Rita. Even the 'black widows' waved and smiled. Katya was transformed, smiling and mischievous. There was nothing ostentatious, nothing forced: a loving kiss on the cheek, smiles and much Polish chatter.

Fred Cox sat quietly in the background, pleased and proud of the part he had played in this outcome. He spent the evening playing chess and enjoying the company of Jane Appleby. When not sitting amongst the group at the large table, Fred and Jane would sit together: their friendship grew. To some, it might appear an odd match: Fred, unrefined, blunt, man of few words, Jane, elegant, eloquent and gentle. Yet, they bonded: Fred smiled in her company, he chatted, an activity he had never really indulged in. This elegant lady softened him: he would lean forward, intimately, sharing quiet conversation. For her part, Jane liked Fred's honesty. When he smiled, which was rare away from her company, it was genuine. His heavy jowls and ponderous features would transform into an amiable, cuddly bear. For the first time in his life he had the time and inclination to make small talk. It was restricted, however, to somebody whose company he enjoyed.

After evening beverage, Fred showered, put on his pyjamas, dressing gown and incontinence pants and walked along the corridor back to his room. As he passed an open doorway to one of the rooms an urgent voice hissed: "Fred, Fred, here!"

Fred was startled by the urgency of the voice. He peered into the dimly lit room: he could make out a figure lying on the bed in pyjamas and dressing gown. In the gloom of the bedside lamp, the gaunt, cadaverous face was recognisable: it was Maurice.

"Come in, Fred, come in."

Fred stood in the doorway, reluctant to enter.

"Please, Fred, come in." The voice was quiet but insistent.

Fred was uneasy, uncomfortable and looked along the corridor hoping someone would come along. The corridor was empty.

Maurice had been ailing for some time. He had noticeably withered over the period since the revelation about his cancer. His handsome features had become gaunt, his thick mane of hair had lost any remaining blond streaks and swamped his thin face; the aquiline nose now seemed almost grotesque. He had become more and more withdrawn, even Spike failed to elicit any humour from him. He had, of course, refused treatments. The best efforts of Rose Richardson and his friends had failed to change his mind. He lay on the bed, his eyes looking abnormally large.

"Shut the door, Fred, draw the chair up."

Fred hated intimate personal situations: he could deal one to one with business people but not this. He pulled a chair reluctantly to the bedside and sat. He focused his attention on the window, a painting, anything but Maurice.

"I've had a few accidents, Fred; they want me to wear those panties. I can't bear it, I won't do it."

"Join the bloody club," Fred said, pulling on the waistband of his nappy: "if I can wear them, you can." Fred spoke sharply.

"No, that's it for me, I'm done." His voice was weak, but firm. "I don't want to be washed, dressed and fed."

Fred sat in silence. He knew Maurice was quite ill; he was shocked, though, by his gaunt features. His breathing was shallow; his bony ribcage rose and fell rapidly. His pyjama top was loose and looked two sizes too big.

Fred started to rise: "I'll get one of the girls to look in," he spoke gruffly but gently.

"No, stay here!" Maurice grasped Fred's thick wrist with his long fingers, gripping tightly.

Fred sat down, startled by his insistence.

"On the dressing table is a business card for Nat Goldman, he owes me big time, Fred. He promised to come and see that lad, Rose's son, when he next performed: he didn't. He won't come unless he's pinned down, Fred; I know you're the man to tackle him. I know you can do it: you could make him listen, you wouldn't put up with his excuses and bluster. Will you do it?"

Maurice's voice was pleading, but he leaned forward, eyes fixed on Fred, demanding. Fred gazed back at him impassively, mouth set. Maurice's gaze didn't falter and after a few moments Fred nodded silently. Maurice fell back on the pillow exhausted but satisfied. After a few minutes he spoke quietly, this time his eyes looked into the distance.

"What's your opinion on the afterlife, Fred? You must have thought about it. What do you think?" Maurice forced a smile: "I know I'll get no bullshit from you."

Fred was out of his comfort zone and for a while didn't speak: he struggled to respond. The silence was hard to bear. He suddenly thought of his conversations with Josh and Lionel. He began to fashion a response: initially, he mumbled, but gradually, gaining confidence, he spoke with more assurance.

"Well, this is what I think, not that anybody knows. I can't bring myself to believe in paradise, heaven, whatever: all that's not for me. I think when you snuff it, your body rots, gets burnt, whatever. Some clever folk say our molecules, atoms, fly off and make new life and new things. Your bits might be in birds, animals, a new person, maybe a star in the sky."

Fred's gruff midland accent contrasted with his new-found eloquence. Maurice lay quietly, eyes closed, listening: surprisingly he found words from blunt Fred Cox soothing.

"On the other hand, you could follow Father Murphy or Rev. Tom. They're good blokes, it has to be said, and they put a good case forward: very comforting if you can believe."

Maurice's features had relaxed and he spoke calmly: "I fancy their way, Fred, I'd like to follow their beliefs, but I've been such a selfish bastard, I don't know whether I'd stand a chance."

Fred thought for a while, then, feeling more comfortable, he spoke from the heart.

The door opened slightly and Denise peeped in. She paused for a moment listening and then quietly closed the door.

"You're not a bad bloke, Spike says so, and he's a good judge of character. You might have been a bullshitter, but there are worse arses in this world. There's no nastiness in you: you wouldn't murder anybody. You're a bit shallow, but that's no real crime."

Fred, as ever blunt and tactless, yet to Maurice, his words carried weight. In his own bluff way Fred was a comfort, he could be trusted and believed.

He continued: "now take me. I've been a miserable sod; I've spent every living moment concentrating on business.

Neglected my family, noticed nothing round me, never smelt the flowers, never looked at the birds, never watched children play, never played make-believe. What does that make me?" Fred paused, both he and Maurice digesting what he had said. It was almost a confessional as much as comfort for Maurice. He continued; words flowed out of him: Maurice lay still, serene, the anguish had disappeared from his face; his hands were clasped over his bony chest. It was if he was a child listening to a comforting bedside story. Fred continued, pouring out his life story and regrets.

It was way past midnight when Denise, again, opened the door: Fred was slumped in his chair, snoring gently. Maurice lay peaceful, sleeping quietly, very quietly. She touched his forehead, it was cold. She felt for a pulse, his wrist and hand were cold, lifeless. She closed the door softly and ran to call Rose Richardson.

Rose entered the room with Denise, checked Maurice and concurred with Denise's assessment. She conferred with her and Denise left to make arrangements, whilst Rose gently wakened Fred from his slumber.

"Come on, Fred. I think we need a good cup of coffee."

Fred rose unsteadily, guided by Rose. They walked down the corridor through the hall to her office. Over a hot sweet coffee, she broke the news to Fred: the news was a shock but, in truth, he wasn't really surprised.

35

Fred missed breakfast: it was dinner before he appeared. He looked weary. He sat down by Jane; she clasped his arm, looking concernedly into his eyes. Nobody spoke: Rose Richardson, having seen Fred enter the dining room, walked in and stood at the end of the table.

"I know everybody will have heard about Maurice. It's a shock. I'd just like to say, I think it's what he would have wanted in the circumstances, a peaceful ending. He was fortunate to have a companion during his final hours and this person won't thank me for mentioning this but nevertheless, thank you, Fred for your kind attention and compassion."

For a moment there was silence and then Jane patted Fred on the back. "Well done, Fred."

Fred's companions nodded in agreement and George shook his hand. Fred was discomforted, slightly embarrassed, an unusual response from him: "I didn't volunteer for it." He was defensive: "I just got trapped."

The solemn atmosphere dissipated and dinner was consumed: more in celebration of Maurice than in the sadness of his passing. After dinner was finished, the group sat reminiscing: there was laughter over Maurice's foibles and mishaps.

As friends lapsed into contemplation, Spike mused on their situation: "our band's getting smaller, where will we end up?"

Lionel, ever pragmatic voiced his opinion: "fear not, as they carry us out of the back door, replacements come in the front. It's not a production line, more a termination line."

"That's right, cheer us up, why don't you?" Spike grimaced,

"Think I'll be buried," George settled his future without qualms.

"Down at the jam factory, I shouldn't wonder," Spike laughed. "What do you prefer Mary?" Spike turned and spoke to Mary at the table behind: "buried or burned?"

Mary's bright eyes were fixed on Spike. She moved her index finger from side to side.

"Neither eh?" Spike gave her a 'thumbs up': "I don't blame you."

The banter continued: it was a defence, a shield against the reality of mortality. Whatever they faced wasn't so bad, they could cope. Jane thought how lucky they were to have companions. They could discuss and find humour in matters of life and death: people living on their own didn't have this release, worries and burdens could mar people's final years.

In the afternoon Lawrence and Mercedes visited. Katya met them at the front door and ushered them into Rose Richardson's office: Rose informed them of Maurice's demise and the part Fred had played in last night's events.

Each time they visited they were more surprised by Fred's changing character, they could hardly believe it was the same Fred.

"I have to say, he was wonderful in his gruff way: I think Maurice would have been comforted by Fred's openness".

"Bluntness you mean," Lol laughed.

"Well, from what Denise heard, Fred put on a good show: of course he wouldn't want us to think that."

Lol and Mercedes found Fred and Jane sitting in the veranda chatting. Jane politely stood to leave, but Fred restrained her, reassuring her it was fine to stay. Jane looked at Lol and Mercedes anxiously, but Mercedes welcomed her.

"Any friend of Fred's is a friend of ours."

"Yes, he hasn't got many," Lol jibed.

"Less of it!" Fred complained.

Mercedes was delighted with Fred's friendship. She was hard-nosed like her father but was pleased at the transformation in him. He was still the old, blunt, pragmatic Fred, but there was humour and a softening of his hard edges. Fred asked about business and Lol filled him in on any developments. Fred listened keenly but respectfully: he trusted Lol implicitly these days and never criticised. If asked for advice, he would discuss as an equal. Lawrence let slip that Mercedes had been away for the weekend with the Brownies: "Brown Owl, now, you know."

"Oh, good for you," Jane was enthusiastic: "I used to do it myself years ago. Takes quite a bit of your time but it's very rewarding."

Mercedes smiled with pleasure: Fred was quietly pleased for her. Mercedes and Jane chatted amiably; they got on well. Lol chipped in now and again with Fred nodding and grunting when required.

"I hear you sat in with someone last night, dad." It was rare that Mercedes referred to her father other than Fred.

Fred Just nodded but Jane spoke up: "he was wonderful, no matter what he says, it was very compassionate, nobody should die alone. It was very kind of him."

Fred's discomfort was broken by Tadeusz arriving and greeting Katya.

"I think your father's had a hand in that romance and that's wonderful too," Jane touched Fred's hand.

As Katya and Tadge greeted each other in Polish, Albert, who was seated in the hall, proclaimed, in a broad midland accent: "Why doh thay spayke English?"

This caused much mirth. 'Miss Faversham', the retired headmistress, tutted to her companions and peered at Albert over her specs. She shook her head sadly, a wry smile on her face.

"Six of the best for you, Albert," Lionel shouted: "a few English lessons wouldn't go amiss, what say you, Miss Lewis?"

'Miss Faversham' couldn't suppress a smile and bowed her head in agreement.

"That's Geoff Bartlett's mate, isn't it Fred? Lol asked.

"Yes, a bloody good bloke, considering he's a foreigner. She could do far worse than him.

"Well, that is a compliment," Jane teased.

After the visitors left, Jane and Fred joined the others for tea. Conversation centred round Maurice and what would happen at his funeral: Maurice had no one that they knew about. They vowed they would give him a good send-off from The Laurels, no matter what.

Fred pulled the card out of his pocket, the one from Maurice's dressing table. He read the gold, embossed inscription, *'Nat Goldman, Manager to the Stars.'* He frowned, thinking of the promise he'd committed to. He had to deliver.

36

Fred stepped out sniffing the air. Even without the lure of a cigarette and coffee, he enjoyed the routine. The autumn air chilled. He was 'rugged up' in his overcoat and scarf. Wood pigeons flapped about on the ivy-covered wall, devouring the dark berries: the path bore witness; purple droppings littered the ground beneath. The resident Jackdaws competed noisily with a group of Magpies: the two gangs swaggered and bickered on the lawn. First the Magpies sallied forth, then the Jackdaws regrouped scattering their rivals, juicy worms seemed to be the prize.

Fred stood for a moment watching the shenanigans, there was something about the crow family: Fred decided they were all robbers, couldn't trust any of them. Josh had told him how they plundered the nests of smaller birds: sad to see when a pair had devoted so much time and energy into raising young. Mind, as he pointed out, they robbed each other's nests as well. No honour amongst thieves.

Fred's interaction with nature was purely down to Josh, plus the fact that he now had the time to observe. For decades business had filled his mind, now, late in life, his mind was free to wander.

Fred rounded the corner as Josh was pouring the coffee: it steamed in the cold air. Even though it was flask coffee, the aroma was irresistible. Fred would have drunk it from an old jam jar. He sat in the old battered chair and Josh handed him the mug, it was the best drink of the day. Along with the roll-up and Josh's company it was also the best part of the day. Conversation turned to Maurice's demise and Fred unburdened himself.

Josh may not have known it but he was, perhaps, the only person to whom Fred revealed his inner thoughts. Betty had scurried round to tell the news to Josh. He was aware of the facts of Maurice's passing, but patiently sat listening to Fred.

"He'd got nobody, not a soul. Fancy, he asked me to sit in with him. I used to think he was an arsehole," Fred paused, contemplating. "He wasn't so bad though: there are worse people than him."

They puffed their cigarettes in silence. Josh quiet, waiting for Fred to resume.

"Do you know, I'm convinced he decided to die; said he would. He just lay down and did it, willed it! I'd heard people say it happens, never believed it, till now. I made him a promise, I don't know why. I said I'd contact that agent bloke he worked for, sounds like a sharp piece of work to me. He vowed to come and listen to Rose's son performing, he never came. All the years Maurice worked for him, he got him out of a many a scrape, I believe, that's the thanks he got: I doubt if he'll come to the bloody funeral. Rose's lad has got talent, not that I'm a connoisseur."

Josh nodded vigorously. "There's no doubt about it, young Dan is good."

"There's more," Fred said, looking awkward: "we talked about dying, religion and all that stuff. Christ, to me! Let the bloody preachers do the job, not me! He said he'd like to have a service with Rev. Tom or Father Murphy: it's put me on the spot." Fred lapsed into silence, having said his piece and waited for Josh's response.

Josh leant forward, elbows on knees and drew on his roll-up. He stifled a smile, picturing Fred receiving Maurice's confession.

"Well, Fred, it sounds like you've got some business to sort out. I think you can sort the first issue; it's up your street. Find out when the next concert is, when Dan does his thing, and make sure that agent chap comes. You're the man to do it, Fred, you can persuade him; I've got full confidence in you. It would be two good deeds together: you'd be carrying out Lionel's request and giving the lad a leg up. As for the second issue, well, if I was you, I'd have a talk to Rose. I'd tell her what Maurice had discussed, concerning Rev. Tom and Father Murphy; I'd wager she'd do the business there. She'd have a chat to both. I think they'd resolve it together, they're good chaps. She's got more tact than you. I tell you what Fred, all these good deeds? You'll be sitting in the confessional soon, doling out Hail Marys. It's definitely a grandstand seat in the next world for you."

"Bollocks," Fred growled. "Hey up, here's Robin. Get that bloody seed out and pour some more coffee."

"Certainly, Sir, right away, Sir," Josh bowed as he reached for the seed tin.

37

In the hallway, close to the door stood the coffin. It rested on a chrome, wheeled byre. On it was a single wreath of mixed flowers with a small white card. It read – *'With Fondest Memories from Your Friends at The Laurels.'*

Father Murphy conducted the short funeral service. Sitting and standing were as many staff and residents as could be accommodated in the hall. Some residents watched from the lounge through the open door.

Before the final prayers, Father Murphy called upon Spike to say a few words. Spike wheeled his chair to the end of the coffin and spoke as if to Maurice. It was a eulogy, simple and unrehearsed. Spike wore a bright Hawaiian style shirt with a small straw trilby on his shaved head, his earring and tattoos were a contrast to Father Murphy's dark attire. The priest gave him a reassuring smile.

Spike doffed his trilby and spoke with sincerity. His Cockney accent, as Fred called it, lent lightness to a solemn occasion. He spoke fondly of Maurice mentioning his job as an impresario's right-hand man. He spoke nothing of Maurice's early life because no-one knew anything of it. He laughed as he recalled some of Maurice's exploits at The Laurels, particularly his stint as a care worker. He drew smiles when he related Maurice's insistence on being called 'Maureece'. He rounded off by saying he was honoured to have known Maurice and irrespective of his exploits, he was a good man at heart. He touched the coffin in salute and wheeled his chair back to the group.

Spike received congratulations from his friends, one or two of whom had a tear in their eye. Father Murphy spoke the final prayers and the funeral directors pushed the byre out onto the drive. They hoisted it into the hearse. Behind was a limousine: into this Spike, Fred, Lionel and George sat. Behind, in her own car, was Rose Richardson accompanied by Jane Appleby. The small cortege crept up the drive and out into the road. The crematorium was five miles away. There, a short service and the committal were conducted by the Rev. Tom. This was the service and send- off agreed by the clergymen and Rose. It was unusual, but having heard of Maurice's final words with Fred, the two men of God kindly gave him their best joint ministrations. Maurice had insisted on no gravestone. He requested his ashes scattered on the sea: he wanted to roam the world. Fred had agreed to carry out his request.

Back at The Laurels, at tea, Rev. Tom was chomping on a sandwich. He approached Fred: "I understand you gave succour to a dying man." He beamed, mumbling through a mouthful of sandwich. "He was fortunate to have you there as a friend: dying can be a lonely business. Your kind efforts are to be commended."

Fred grunted, slightly, embarrassed. The whole business had brought, for him, uncomfortable attention.

Spike declared Fred would soon be taking over Rev Tom's work.

"Not bloody likely," Fred shook his head: "that's the last time."

Tea passed with a jovial atmosphere. People alluded to Maurice's passing but conversation always ended with some laughter about the time he did this or said that. For most residents time was short, no good dwelling on death and sadness. Make light of it and have a laugh. If someone was low or maudlin, there were others who were cheerful, spirits could be lifted.

Lionel passed the word round; they were giving Maurice a bit of a send-off; a spot of port and sherry in his and Spike's room at 9-30, after showers. George and Jane agreed, but only for an hour. Fred, maintaining his newfound sociability, also assented.

At 9-30, the group, in their dressing gowns, crowded into Spike and Maurice's room. The resident pair sat on their beds, George and Jane in the easy chairs. Fred dragged a chair in from the corridor. Knowing that drinking would be out of mugs, Jane borrowed a couple of glasses from the kitchen and provided a bottle of coffee liquor. Fred tried a shot of liquor with Jane, he found it pleasant. The others charged their mugs with port and sherry.

Lionel stood up, ramrod straight; "friends, a toast to a fallen comrade. To Maureece, may his memory live on." The friends raised their glasses and toasted a departed friend.

"Down in one, everyone," Spike insisted: "that's what he would have wished."

Even Jane swallowed her drink in one. The mugs and glasses clinked as they were recharged. George surprised all, commenting that Maurice had been a free man: no woman had got their claws into him.

Jane protested, with humour: "beg your pardon, George, lady present."

"Sorry, Jane, you're a real lady, I didn't mean you; no way."

They laughed together, relating amusing tales about Maurice's exploits. It was after eleven when George rose from his chair. "Oops, something wrong with my legs, they've gone wobbly."

Jane stood and making her apologies, bade the remaining men goodnight. She led George out into the corridor, he was mumbling as he went.

"I'll miss Maurice; he was always kind to me: never minded my drumming."

The remaining trio sat quietly, for a while, sipping their drinks: Fred pondered on his promises to Maurice.

"I'll get one of the lads to take his ashes when they travel to the docks."

"Now that's a good final journey, wouldn't mind that myself," Spike said, topping up their mugs. "Where do your lads travel to?"

Fred, who rarely drank, smacked his lips as he drained his mug: he explained enthusiastically how the truckers travelled all over the country and to the continent, taking loads out. He explained the logistics of returning with loads. Lionel and

Spike kept his mug topped up. Fred was swallowing it like pop, having been assured there was no strength in it.

Fred rambled on; Spike and Lionel had never heard him express so many words: it was as if a log jam had been released. They encouraged him, asking questions about trucks and trucking, Spike winking at Lionel. His burbling gradually became slurred: as he struggled with his words, his midland accent became more pronounced and he embellished his narrative with more and more swear words.

"When I started out, I didn't have two halfpennies to rub together; my arse was hanging out my trousers; the first truck I owned was ex-army; one step up from a horse and cart: you mauled your balls off trying to hand crank it. Christ! It broke your bloody arm if it backfired."

He paused, his face red, staring at his companions gormlessly.

"That's interesting, Fred, you had it hard, no doubt about that," Spike's voice grew louder as the drink took effect. He slyly goaded Fred, hoping to get a reaction: "did you have faggots and peas?"

"Faggots and peas? Faggots and pissing peas? Pigs dick and lettuce more like and a scrape of dripping on a crust!"

"What about pudding, Fred?" Lionel kept the momentum going.

"Pudding? Pissing pudding? What pudding? You licked your plate, that's what and sucked your teeth, that was your pudding."

Spike and Lionel could hold out no longer and started tittering.

"What's up with you two? What's so funny?" Fred demanded.

Seeing Fred's scowl, they stifled their mirth: "nothing, Fred."

"Nothing, laughing at bloody nothing?" Fred fixed them with a withering glare.

"Laughing at nothing, Fred, but it was funny all the same," Lionel stifled his laughter and tried to look serious.

Fred stared vacantly at them for several seconds, then: "you pair of bastards, you've bloody led me on!"

His shoulders began to shake. Tears streamed from his eyes and gurgling laughter rose from his throat: they all rocked with hysterical laughter. It culminated in Fred having a coughing fit and chest pain. When it subsided, Fred wiped his eyes, still tittering. "You pair of tosspots!"

Fred had probably never laughed so much, years of restraint were released. Eventually, the hilarity, coupled with alcohol's soporific effect, exhausted the threesome. They sat quietly in mild stupor: occasionally, one would titter setting the others off. Gradually sleep crept upon them.

When Mandy checked after midnight, Fred was snoring in the armchair, Lionel and Spike fast asleep on top of their beds: Mandy noted the bottles and quietly closed the door. In the morning, Katya finally roused the hung-over miscreants at 8-30.

"Who's been naughty boys then and Mr Cox a teetotaller too, tut, tut!" As she left the room she shouted over her shoulder: "runny eggs and greasy bacon for breakfast and serve you right too!"

38

Days merged into weeks and winter inexorably cast its spell. Some mornings, frost coated the trees and lawns: it was a magical visage particularly when viewed from the warmth and security of the care home. Inside, The Laurels' steady beat never faltered, the routine endured. As old residents departed, new residents appeared. Economics ruled that there could be no vacancies: profit margins were tight; replacements were almost immediate and seamless. The cheeriness of Rose and her team masked what was a depressing reality: at The Laurels, life could be short.

The residents' own characters contributed greatly to the atmosphere and well-being of the establishment. Many stayed in their rooms and valued privacy, others withdrew completely, suffering from the loss of a partner or independence. For some, The Laurels could only offer good care and security to see out their days. Of those who sought company and appeared in the public areas, there was a will to make life as pleasant as possible. Able residents did occasionally go for outings, one or two took a taxi; sometimes a friend or relative took them out for dinner or a ride. Most, however, were content to remain at The Laurels: many became anxious when removed from its security; relatives were often perplexed by their refusals to venture out. Fred had, once or twice, been out for dinner with Lawrence and Mercedes. When Jane's daughter had been over, she too had a couple of outings, but like Fred, was content to remain in the home. Lionel and Spike never ventured out except into the garden on fine days.

Spike was trying to engage in conversation with an elderly man. His wife had been resident for only a couple of weeks. At home, she had gradually become weaker and more helpless. It had reached the point where the old man could no longer cope. He was distraught and bereft at having to submit his wife to a care home. Each day, he arrived by public transport, or taxi. He sat with his helpless wife, patting her hand, looking into her eyes and offering drinks to her lips. It was a heartrending sight. He stayed all day, taking his meals at The Laurels at a modest charge.

Spike worried about the man and made a point of engaging him with little snippets of conversation. He tried to distract him from the intense attention he gave to his wife. Spike knew the man would fail himself, if he continued with such intensity. He made small talk with him, being careful to include his wife, even though she showed little response. Spike eventually won the man's trust with his persistence. His technique was to speak to both, with his knack for small talk and banter.

He greeted them thus: "morning Bill, morning Marjorie. How are you both today? What about this weather? Enough to freeze a brass monkey's. You need your winter woollies today Marjorie." Gradually he won the man's respect and attention: he visibly relaxed when Spike was present. He smiled and began to enjoy Spike's chat, even his wife followed Spike with her eyes, her face brightening when he spoke to her.

"He's worth his weight in gold," Lionel commented, watching Spike weaving his magic, "he's worth a couple of trick cyclists anytime."

"Trick cyclists? I've seen a few of them in my time and the wall of death. I used to go to the circus when it came to town: I loved the clowns and the lion tamer."

"He means psychiatrists, George: you know, therapists," Jane explained.

"Oh them: don't have anything to do with them. Don't look into their eyes, my mother used to say, they'll put you into a trance, especially if they get their watches out." His thoughts turned to dinner: "hope it's rice pudding today with some jam."

"Bloody hell, George, wish we were all pleased so easily," Fred grunted. He turned, looking at Mary who was sat behind: "what do you think Mary, rice pudding for you?" It was an innocuous question but remarkable for Fred.

Mary gave him a finger down, Fred persisted: "how about sponge and custard?" Fred got his response, a finger up from Mary: he gave her 'a thumbs up'.

Jane watched him: Fred, the insular, stubbornly independent Fred, had thawed and revealed what she knew had lay hidden under his thick skin. If only things could remain the same and they could all stay together. Lionel, she knew, was in his nineties but looked set to live for years. George? Not so old but fit: sadly, dementia was creeping up on him; as for Spike, he was young and although it was tragic for him to be in a 'home', he would thrive. What of Fred and herself: what might their futures hold? She put it from her mind.

The call went up for dinner: it was a major event. Mealtimes were punctual: residents, particularly dementia sufferers, were rooted to routines and time. The tedium of confinement was broken by mealtimes, clocks were watched and anticipation rose as the dining hour approached. Staff would begin transporting the less able to the dining room before the appointed hour. It was a meeting point for social integration, particularly for those who didn't mix easily: for some there was little conversation, but recognition and a smiling face was sufficient.

"Hope it's not peas today," George expressed a concern that many shared. Peas had a habit of rolling across the table and onto the floor. Another moan occurred when meat required chewing: with age came a need for soft food, the ability to masticate and bite decreased. George was often heard to enquire whether he could get his false teeth sharpened.

Today, however, pudding dominated his thoughts, returning inevitably to his favourite: "hope there's jam with it."

Rita joined the conversation: "well, I fancy apple pie, I hope it's apple pie. I don't want any jam with it, especially if it's raspberry with seeds in it: they get under your teeth. No, let's have custard."

She sang the school kid's rhyme: "spatter, spatter custard, green snot pie, all washed down with a dead dog's eye."

"Mind, if it's jam with seeds, George, you just do this:-" she took her teeth out, holding them in the palm of her hand, cackling with delight.

'Miss Faversham' peered over her glasses at Rita, frowning and tutting. She rose from her chair with the widows: they made their way to the dining room shaking their heads at a gleeful Rita as they passed.

39

As December crept forward, Christmas decorations appeared. A tree stood in the hall, adorned with baubles, tinsel and lights. The days were busy: Father Murphy visited with the church choir, festive entertainment was laid on; a cheerful atmosphere prevailed.

Reverend Tom visited: he recited a seasonal chapter from Dickens; this was typical of the amiable vicar. He interspersed this with some seasonal bible readings and chats with the residents.

"How do you square all this?" Spike asked Lionel: "you being an atheist and all."

"I don't mind it at all: I like the hymns, I don't even mind the readings. There's something comforting about them even if you're a non-believer: mind, I wouldn't have said that when I was younger. Spreading good ethics and behaviour is fine; the trouble begins when propaganda and war, in the name of religion, rear their ugly heads."

Reverend Tom finished his reading, looking round with his toothy grin. He stepped back and toppled backwards over his chair. The 'black widows' rushed forward to assist him, fussing over him, brushing him down: he bounced up beaming, nodding apologies to the room. George spotted his odd socks, one patterned, one plain. Spike and Lionel tittered: the vicar's eccentricity and clumsiness were renowned.

Rita piped up: "I nearly saw your bits then, vicar, but I looked away."

"How very gracious, Rita, so very kind." Rev. Tom strode off, still beaming: he had a rendezvous with a sandwich in the kitchen.

Saturday, after dinner, the Brownies rolled up: they marched through the hall to the far end. They formed two rows, smaller girls at the front. Brown Owl, Mrs Belshaw, sat at the piano: they struck up with 'Deck the Halls', they sang with vigour, faces eager, proud to be performing. As usual the residents loved the girls and their singing. The Brownies' pride and the thrill of performing made for some amusing facial expressions: some girls were wide-eyed, trying to look earnest; some mouthed their words with exaggerated expressions. They raised their faces reverently to the roof; others looked round shyly at the residents, watching their reactions.

This year, as well as a couple of mums assisting, a second Brown Owl helped usher in the girls: it was Mercedes. She gave Fred a wave as she marched in. She stood to the side: from time to time she guided a girl to the toilet and back, kids being kids, no sooner had one returned, than another put their hand up to go. Mercedes took it in her stride with patience, obviously enjoying her role.

Carols and other festive songs filled the hall. After a joyous spell of singing, Mercedes beckoned the girls to sit: they sat cross legged whilst one of the older girls recited a seasonal feel-good story. Finally, a rousing 'Sleigh Bells' rounded off the concert: everyone applauded vigorously. The girls were flushed with pride. Maisie and Betty emerged from the kitchen with trays of fairy cakes and squash: the girls gathered round excitedly.

Fred, sitting with Jane, was quietly proud of Mercedes and watched amused. A Brownie, with long black hair came skipping across to where they sat, smiling and flicking her hair back with one hand the other clutched a fairy cake. She stood in front of them: Fred recognised her immediately it was 'his Brownie'. She slid on the floor doing the splits, flicking her hair back and watching their reaction.

"Oh, very good," Jane said, "my, you are flexible."

She handed a startled Fred, a half-eaten fairy cake with the command, "Don't eat it!"

She raised her arms over her head and bent backwards into a crab position: she held the position until Jane exclaimed: "well done, well done; that's very good, isn't it Fred?"

Fred couldn't help but smirk and nodded vigorously. The girl stood up, proud, flicking her long hair: she chomped on her retrieved cake, glancing from one to the other, revelling in the adulation.

"We like to sing to old people, especially if they are sad: mum says it brings a bit of cheer into their lives."

After the refreshments, Mrs Bellshaw clapped her hands and the girls gathered round her: they formed into pairs and marched out to lively applause. Mercedes brought up the rear, smiling contentedly at Jane and Fred. Everyone, Brownies and residents, benefitted from the experience, there was hardly a resident who didn't feel lifted by it.

After tea, Fred and Jane sat in the veranda chatting: most of the others remained in the dining room. Mary was seated in her wheelchair in the veranda doorway, sideways on: Mavis had pushed her in to watch the dying embers of the day, at the same time she could see and be seen from the dining room. Jane asked Mary how she was and received a raised finger for ok. Since Spike's successful tutoring with finger talk, everybody interacted with Mary.

Jane left to fetch her book, leaving Fred and Mary: Fred commented on the dark evenings, getting an affirmation from Mary's raised finger. Mary's bright eyes watched Fred: he asked if Mary liked winter and received a finger down as a no, Fred agreed with her, all the while Mary's eyes were fixed on Fred.

Suddenly, a blinding pain seared into Fred's forehead: he gasped with the intensity of it, his face contorted. He writhed in his seat, gasping for his breath; he slid off the chair onto his knees, looking desperately at Mary. He toppled to the floor, on his side, grunting with the pain. He struggled to draw air into his lungs. All the while, Mary's eyes never left him: she was fixed, as ever, in her sitting position, able only to move her eyes and her fingers.

Lionel was sitting in the dining room, his back to the veranda, opposite sat Spike in his wheelchair. They were discussing euthanasia, a topic often raised: Lionel's view was it should be legal if a sufferer requested it, Spike wasn't so sure. They debated back and forth. Occasionally, Spike leant to the side, checking on Mary: he had spotted her interaction with Fred and Jane who sat out of view. He argued a point with Lionel then peeped across at Mary.

Mary's position hadn't changed, of course, but now her eyes were strained to their extremity at the side, looking at Spike. He noticed the change, waved and carried on with his discussion. The next time he looked, Mary's eyes were still fixed on him: this time Spike noticed her finger moving side to side animatedly, he knew this was Mary's way of trying to attract attention. He shouted across to her: "everything all right Mary?" Mary dropped her finger, a no.

Spike was puzzled: he had seen Jane leave the veranda but knew Fred was sitting round the corner. "Do you need some help Mary?" his voice was loud enough for Fred to hear, unless he'd dozed off. Mary immediately responded with a raised finger, a yes.

Still perplexed, Spike wheeled his chair to the veranda door: "what's the trouble Mary?"

As soon as Spike pushed into the doorway, he spotted Fred, prone, sprawled on the floor: his face blue and twisted. "Oh God, shout for help somebody, Fred's collapsed. Quick!"

Katya was working the afternoon shift: she heard the call and ran into the veranda, Mavis followed. Katya rolled Fred onto his back and commenced C.P.R.: Mavis rang 999 for an ambulance. Spike rushed to Rose Richardson's office, she grabbed a defibrillator and ran to the veranda. Lionel pushed

Mary back into the dining room and out into the lounge with the remaining residents.

Peering through the dining room doorway, Jane stood tearful, face riven with anxiety. She clung to Spike's arm fearing the worst: she knew it was going to be bad.

40

The Jaguar swept smoothly up the drive, the crunch of the gravel was the only indication of its movement. It drew to a halt before The Laurels' front door. The smartly dressed, middle-aged woman emerged from the front passenger door: as she opened the rear door, she was joined by the tall driver.

"Come on, let's give you a lift out," the driver reached out his arms to the figure in the back seat.

"Piss off and give me some room. Pass me the bloody sticks."

The speech was slurred but the accent and language were unmistakeable.

"Bloody hell, Fred, you're stubborn. You're supposed to be in a bloody wheelchair: you should still be in hospital by rights."

"Never mind all that, give me some bloody space."

Slowly, very slowly, the stocky figure swivelled round on his seat and planted his feet on the gravel. He paused puffing, blowing his cheeks out. Placing his walking sticks into the gravel, he braced himself with a mighty effort: red-faced, he heaved himself into a standing position and leant on the car, drained.

"I'm going to fetch you a wheelchair."

"No you're not. I'm not going in a bloody wheelchair, if it takes all afternoon, I'm not going in one."

"God you're bloody awkward," Mercedes strode to the front door and rang the bell.

Lawrence knew it was no use intervening and stood behind his father-in-law ready to support or catch him if necessary. Fred moved slowly towards the front door: he took small steps, leading all the time with his right leg. His left arm was also weak; he had hoisted himself up with one good arm and leg. As he reached the steps the front door opened, Rose Richardson and Mandy, the plump carer, stood before him.

"Hello, Fred, welcome back." Rose had observed his strenuous efforts, his limp and the droop on the left side of his face. He puffed and blew with the effort. Rose could see his drawn features and also his weight loss: his collar seemed loose round his normal bull neck.

"We'll just stand beside you as you come up the steps, just to steady you."

This time, Fred didn't protest and was grateful for their support.

From the moment of arrival, faces had been gathering at windows, studying him, assessing the damage, assessing his chances. The group passed through the hall, Rose asked if he wanted to go to his room for respite, Fred refused and they entered the lounge slowly.

A cheer went up from his friends as they tried to hide the shock at the legacy of his stroke.

"Come on, Fred, sit down here, give me your sticks: take the weight off your feet." Everybody was eager to chip in with comments, making him welcome.

"Tea and biscuits in a minute, Fred:" to George, food cured everything.

Fred stood for a moment looking round and drawing breath: his eyes alighted on someone to his right. He moved slowly and painfully across: he bent and with great tenderness kissed the person on the cheek. He looked into her eyes: "thank you."

Mary's eyes watched him. Her finger moved slowly from side to side: that meant thank you or ok. Fred smiled at her and limped back to his chair; he flopped down exhausted, but felt at home.

Mercedes and Lawrence, having delivered their difficult charge, followed Rose to her office for tea, tactics and words of comfort. Fred had remained in hospital four days only: he discharged himself, stating he wasn't going to die there. Pills and blood-thinning drugs were the order of the day, along with lifestyle changes: none of these appealed to Fred. The prognosis, that he might regain some movements with time, was countered by the fact he could have a further stroke or heart attack. Fred appeared to accept it; the concerns were left to Mercedes and Lol.

Back in the lounge, George stood up: he, personally, fetched two custard creams for Fred from the trolley.

"You've got it made, Fred: all this attention. There are some benefits," Spike chirped.

"Not bloody many," Fred grumbled: his words were slurred but intelligible.

There was an awkward moment of silence when Rita shouted out: "there's something wrong with your face, Fred."

It was broken by Fred shouting back: "there's always been something wrong with my face, Rita. It's bloody ugly."

There was laughter, Fred had a crooked smile. Any awkwardness was gone, the situation was accepted.

Jane, who had been resting in her room, entered the lounge, halting as she spotted Fred. She walked up to him tears springing from her eyes: she noted his sticks and his dropped facial features. She hurried over to him and kissed his cheek.

"Oh, Fred, we thought we'd lost you."

"No bloody fear," Fred spoke softly, "not just yet anyway." He gazed up fondly at Jane; he studied her face intently and her own slight facial droop.

"You know, Jane, we're a good match; a pair of bloody book-ends."

41

Josh sat back in his chair thinking. He knew about Fred's collapse: he knew the details; he knew he might never recover. He pondered on the fickleness of life, its ups and downs. He had been at The Laurels long enough: he had seen people come and go; this was the reality, the cycle of life. This was Fred, though, it was different: he and Fred were close, at least Josh thought so. He drew on his cigarette: he knew Fred's health wasn't good, but his robust character distracted from it. He thought about his own modest tobacco consumption: he'd promised the family he'd stop; maybe this was a good time to start.

A scraping noise disrupted his thoughts. He listened again: there it was; he turned puzzled. Visible through the bare shrubbery was a figure, moving along the path, on two sticks: it was Fred.

Josh couldn't believe his eyes: struggling slowly, blowing his cheeks out, Fred progressed. The scraping sound was his left foot dragging along the gritty surface. Josh jumped up concerned: a few days ago Fred was at death's door, now he was dragging himself to his morning liaison. Josh moved forward to help him: "Hell's bells, Fred, you shouldn't be here. What are you thinking of?"

"Shut up, stand back and get my pissing chair," the slurred speech was noticeable but the venom was still there.

A surprised Josh grabbed the battered old chair and pushed it behind Fred who dropped into it like a stone. Josh was concerned, but after a few rasping breaths Fred held his hand out: "Coffee."

Josh poured a mug and handed it over; Fred grasped it in his right hand, his left slowly and shakily rose to steady it. Josh stood for a couple of minutes while Fred sipped his drink.

"That's good," Fred relaxed, "that's bloody good." His breathing slowed: he looked at Josh with a steady gaze, his eyes wider than normal, "Come on, fag!"

"Is that wise?" Josh protested.

"Listen here," Fred interrupted," I haven't mauled my guts out, struggling round here, for nothing. Come on, light up."

Josh gave up: he could have refused, but what difference would it make now? He lit up a cigarette and handed to Fred. They savoured their nicotine, looking across at each other: Fred had a small smile which was twisted due to his affliction, "I'm a bloody invalid now."

"I can see that," Josh said softly.

Fred drew on his cigarette and blew out the smoke slowly: "What with that and pissy pants. Christ Almighty!"

They looked at each other, Fred resignedly and Josh sympathetically. They couldn't maintain their gravity and both started to titter; Josh blew his roll-up out of his mouth.

"It seems a poor time to be laughing Fred."

"You're wrong: it's the right bloody time."

The crunch of fast footsteps made them turn round; looming into view was Rose Richardson and Mavis.

"I couldn't stop him, Mrs Richardson; he said he had to go out."

"I know that, Mavis, don't worry." Rose confronted Fred: "so, your treatment's started eh, a fag and coffee."

Fred didn't speak: Josh was on his feet apologising.

"Look, Fred's got a mind of his own, I don't blame you Josh. We were just worried he would fall: he's still weak. Mind, not weak enough to miss a fag," she looked down sternly at Fred.

Fred spoke slowly and quietly: "look, Rose, this is medicine to me: it's better than all the pills and potions. It's a bit late in life for me to change. It's not just a fag and a coffee: I enjoy a half hour with this man, he puts up with me."

Josh was touched: he felt close to Fred, there was a bond.

Rose smiled grimly: "well, you may be right. Probably too late to change a lifetime's habits, may as well die happy, eh. Come on, Mavis, it's a lost cause." She patted him on the shoulder: "just make sure he gets back safe, Josh." With that she took Mavis by the arm and walked back towards the house.

A movement caught Fred's eye: "hey, old pal, come and join us: you don't mind if I'm an invalid, do you?"

The robin twisted its head, watching Fred: it waited for its reward. Fred tossed some seed on the ground, the bird fluttered down pecking around his feet.

"Don't let that bloody Magpie find your nest this spring." He turned back to Josh: "I thought I was invincible, once, tackle anything, anybody. Now, I don't think I've much time left and I'm bloody useless, a cripple."

Josh paused for a while in his steady, thoughtful way: "cripple's can do plenty, Fred. Look at Franklin Roosevelt and that Stephen Hawking: it didn't quell their spirit. Look at Robin Redbreast: last year the sparrowhawk killed his mate. Has it floored him? Well, it did, but he's bounced back. He'll be gearing up in spring with new plumage: he'll strut his stuff, looking for a new mate. Meanwhile, he's building his strength scoffing our seed."

Fred spoke as if to Josh and the robin: "we don't mind him eating our seed: he causes us no bother. Not only that, he's always pleased to see us rain or shine, happy, miserable or even bloody crippled. How many people can you say that about?"

"True, Fred, very true. If you're at one with Nature, life's burdens don't seem so bad and we can face it, we three.

42

In the dining room, a ruckus was developing: Rita had accused a resident of stealing her slippers. The recipient of her wrath, a tall thin woman with wide eyes, denied the offence and called her a liar. Katya hurried to diffuse the situation: she had dealt with the combatants in the past when they almost came to blows.

"Ladies, ladies please, come, let us sort this problem out."

Mixed up laundry was a perpetual problem: clothes were labelled but problems still arose. Laundry staff delivered to the wrong rooms, toileting accidents occurred, emergency clothing sometimes had to be found in a hurry. Coupled with these problems, some demented residents would wander into another's rooms and filch an item they fancied. Relatives were annoyed to discover a new cardigan worn by someone else, while the true owner could be wearing a tatty garment. It called for much diplomacy on the part of the staff to smooth things out.

Spike and Lionel were tittering about the time Maurice's pants were on Albert. Spike related the tale with relish.

"They were those skimpy briefs, you know, barely covered your bits. Not only that, they had a shark's head print: the teeth surrounded the fly hole. Maurice was not amused when he spotted Albert coming out of the bathroom. They were his best 'pulling pants': it didn't help that Albert's bits were poking out everywhere. He threw them away when he got them back."

Lionel guffawed: "he couldn't compete with Albert."

Jane fussed over Fred. Since his stroke she was very attentive. She wiped a toast crumb from his mouth with a napkin: Fred, who normally hated fuss, offered no resistance. People lingered in the dining room, chatting, sipping their beverages. Fred was distracted and pensive, looking into the distance.

"What's wrong?" George peered concernedly into Fred's eyes. His mild dementia hadn't diminished his sensitive nature.

Fred, who one time would have told him to mind his own business, responded amiably. He expressed his concern about getting Dan an audition: it weighed heavily on him. "I promised Maurice and time's slipping away."

Spike considered Nat Goldman an untrustworthy companion: "he doesn't give a toss about anybody, not even Maurice, as far as I can see."

Fred agreed with him: Nat Goldman seemed an arse, but he'd made a promise.

"Why don't you persuade him to call in for the entertainment afternoon, next week: Dan's putting on a show for us."

The group agreed with Jane's suggestion, they had no faith in a result but the suggestion was reasonable.

"Tell him I'm on the drums and it's nearly Christmas," George beamed.

Spike thought it a lost cause.

A rippling sound rent the air. "Oops, Jacks vacated his bowels: to the lounge everybody." The group rose scraping their chairs, they followed Lionel. Fred made his excuses and made slow progress across the hall to his room. He had mastered his walking sticks with their arm supports but his leg dragged across the floor. His left arm remained weak and the effort required caused him chest pains. Rose and her girls made sure he took his medication but he never mentioned the pains: he wanted no more hospital visits.

He slumped into his armchair, closed his eyes for a few minutes and recovered his strength. He fished in his jacket pocket for the card Maurice had given him. He studied the gold script: *'Nat Goldman Impresario, agent to the stars.'* "Wanker," Fred thought. He keyed the phone number into his mobile and sat while it rang. He had no rehearsed plan; he would play it by ear: this was always Fred's way. A secretary answered, Mr Goldman was apparently busy, but she would take a message. Fred knew it would be consigned to the bin and pressed on.

"Look, this is important. Big money could be involved here. Get him on." Fred knew how people like Goldman worked.

Nat Goldman spoke: "I'm busy, what do you want?"

Fred was on his mettle: his speech although slurred was strong, he wasted no time with small talk.

"Right, you promised a friend you would visit him, to audition a lad. You broke your promise, you never came. I'm talking about Maurice. Me? I'm Fred Cox. I want to talk business and I can't do with bullshit. The lad's good, there's money to be made so why don't you get off your arse? Maurice is dead and gone; you didn't come to see him. Don't give me any shite, you owe him, he did plenty for you. The least you can do is to get your arse down here: he's putting a show on, Friday, at two-o clock. Look, give the lad half an hour of your time. I keep my promises; I promised Maurice on his deathbed that I would contact you and I've done it. You've got an opportunity, seize it or piss off and live with your conscience. Do the decent thing for once: you can pay back a debt and stand a good chance of making some money. It's in your hands."

Fred said his piece and slumped back in his chair. He thought Goldman would respond more to money than honour: he knew his type. He lay back, spent: "I gave it my best shot Maurice, now I'm buggered".

When Jane looked in later, Fred was snoring. She picked up the calling card off the floor and read it. She knew Fred would have made a good effort, no half measures: she hoped it would bear fruit.

43

Betty entered the front door as Fred exited for his morning constitutional. She let him out, poking him in the chest: "smoking kills."

"Yes, and your rock cakes."

"Get off before I kick your sticks from under you," She threatened, waving her fist.

Fred struggled down the steps, pausing at the bottom: he struggled for breath. Coming up the drive with her bouncy steps was Katya: she waved as she approached. Her cheeks were rosy and she looked well. She stopped in front of Fred:

"I've got some news, Mr Cox."

"What? You're going back to Poland to give us some peace."

She grasped his brawny hand excitedly: "No. No. You're not getting rid of me that easily. Tadeusz and I have become engaged and it's all thanks to you."

Fred gave an exaggerated frown: "what? You come here, a foreigner, all this way and then you're going to marry another foreigner. What's wrong with a good Englishman?"

"I tried one of them, Mr. Cox, remember? He wasn't so good, eh?"

Fred nodded: "you're right; he was a piece of shite." His voice softened: "you'll make a fine couple. Tadge is a good man and I'm pleased for you."

Katya kissed him on the cheek. "Thanks, Mr. Cox." She bounced up the steps and into The Laurels.

Fred felt contented. He struggled round the corner, grunting with the effort: a pair of chattering magpies seemed to mock him. He glared up at them: "piss off". He made for the rear of the house, his foot dragging. A movement caught his eye, he stopped: it was the robin perched on a twig. It sang, a sweet wistful song. Fred halted, listening: the bird flitted on ahead, stopping every few yards. It waited for him to catch up, it was leading the way, Fred thought. They reached the shed where Josh had already placed the chairs: he was pouring the coffee.

"Pass the seed," Fred watched the robin perched on the roof: it struck up with another short sweet phrase. "Hark, he's singing for us this morning."

Josh emerged with the seed tin: "do you know, the robin is the only bird who sings through the winter. Sometimes a thrush strikes up but Robin is consistent, rain, snow or shine. It's his winter song; they say he's sad because summer's gone. You're honoured getting a personal performance."

Fred beamed: he held out his hand and the robin was straight down perching on his thumb, pecking up the seed. There was an intimacy between man and bird, like old friends.

Eventually, he threw some seed onto the ground as Josh emerged with the coffee.

"You've got a mate there, Fred," Josh puffed on his roll-up.

Fred was particularly attentive this morning, Josh thought. He asked how his good lady was, asked about his lads, especially the youngster.

Josh took pleasure in telling him. Life was pretty good: his wife was happy, his eldest doing well at college and the youngest showing real promise as a football apprentice.

"Sometimes a bit of luck or fate comes your way and you have to embrace it. Mind, you don't believe in that stuff, eh, Fred?"

Fred sat, blowing out smoke, contemplating: "there might just be something in it; perhaps fate does lend a hand sometimes."

"Hey, Fred, you're not softening up, are you?"

"No bloody way."

Nevertheless, when Fred pulled himself up to leave, he surprised Josh, shaking his hand vigorously clasping him with both hands, even the weak left hand. "I've enjoyed your company these mornings," he spoke gruffly but looked Josh straight in the eye, pausing before he turned. He limped along the path leaving a surprised Josh watching him.

After dinner, Lawrence and Mercedes visited. His daughter was eager to impart some news, Fred could tell.

"Well, Fred, what do you think?" She paused, building the suspense.

"Come on, come on," Fred grew exasperated.

"We've only gone and bought out Woodcock's transport, that's what!"

"Bloody hell, bloody hell," Fred punched the air: "Bloody hell, how did you manage it?"

Mercedes explained: Lawrence had heard a rumour about their finances; apparently the son had run up some huge debts. They were on the point of bankruptcy, Lol put in a bid for the business, through a secondary source, and they had no option but to accept. Of course, they didn't know who it was till the deed was done.

"Yes, there is justice!" Fred was red-faced and animated: it culminated in a wracking coughing fit. When it subsided, Fred congratulated them: "you've done bloody well. You're a damn good team. I should have told you years ago, I'm bloody proud of you, both."

Mercedes hugged her father, perhaps the first time since she was a child. Lol stood slightly embarrassed: he'd never seen his father-in-law show emotion or affection. When Mercedes pulled away with a kiss on her father's cheek, Lol shook his hand. There was warmth, they were family.

44

The driver stood patiently as his fare struggled into the rear of the black cab. It was a slow process. He was used to the aged and afflicted and sometimes his patience would be rewarded by a generous tip. Today, however, he wasn't so sure. The old chap looked belligerent. The offer of a helping hand had been shrugged off: worse, his charge wasn't talkative, always a bad sign.

The black cab disappeared out of the gates and away from The Laurels. Fred sat in the back, a determined look on his face. In his pocket he carried a notebook: there was business to attend to.

Back at The Laurels, breakfast was just finishing, residents were either chatting or drifting back to the lounge. Spike was wondering aloud what Fred was up to; nobody seemed to know, not even Jane, in whom Fred often confided.

George suggested he'd run away, didn't like the food perhaps. He added sadly, "But where would he go?"

"Who'd have any of us? We are just inmates in an institution." Lionel was philosophical; "we are washed up, like flotsam and jetsam on an island called The Laurels. We can only leave when they carry us out."

"There are worst places to be washed up on," Spike suggested; "we don't get beaten very often and you get jam and pudding regularly, eh George?"

Jane chipped in: "we've got each other; that counts for such a lot. I think our friendship, together with the staff, makes life bearable. I remember how lonely I was before I came here. We don't want to burden family, they have lives to lead and, for them, life seems hectic and uncertain, these days. We certainly had hard times but life seemed steadier. I don't know if I would cope with the hustle and bustle these days."

Lionel expressed his belief in her abilities: "you'd cope, Jane, no matter what."

Conversation tailed off: they contemplated past lives and their present situation. A melancholy mood drifted over them and they were quieted.

Jane pondered her life as a solicitor's wife. Her marriage wasn't really a love match: true, the partnership was sound and they were content, lucky perhaps. They had been friends and it was convenient, but there had not been that spark, that excitement. It had seemed the norm in the company they kept, not exciting but nothing bad.

Lionel thought about his wife, they had been happy. They met at university: he was older, having served in the war. He resumed his studies when he was demobbed reading History; she, Social Sciences. She had been a firebrand, a left wing Socialist; he, a quiet and earnest student. They seemed polar opposites, yet, love blossomed: they were close and in love throughout their married life. When she passed away at The Laurels, Lionel was devastated: life was empty, the home had saved him. He once contemplated ending it all. Fate, providence, whatever, had partnered him with Spike: it was providential for both. They nursed each other and wounds healed, both emerged from a black abyss, saved. He knew in his heart that without that fortuitous meeting, he would have given up.

Jane shook off her reverie. George was snoring in his chair; head lolling on his chest, Lionel gazed into the distance, deep in thought. Spike was sitting with his head in his hands, an unusual pose for him: usually he was active, chatting, turning this way or that. Jane craned her neck and noticed tears on his cheeks. She rose, concerned, she had never seen Spike low or distressed, ever. She hurried round the table.

Lionel, seeing her concern and haste turned and saw his distraught roommate tearful. Like Jane, he had rarely witnessed Spike anything but cheerful. He put his arm round Spike's shoulders as Jane took his hand.

"Whatever's wrong, old chap?"

Spike struggled with his words. "Talking about family made me realise what a cock-up I've made of my life and my family's. I don't know what's happened to them, or where they are. Are they happy? What happened to my little girl? I've been a fool."

He spoke no more and no amount of consoling could coax out the 'old Spike.' He retired to his room, leaving the others muted.

Jane broke the silence: "I feel so sorry for him, he does so much for other people and now he needs help and there's no-one to help him. I feel helpless and sad."

"I suppose he's thinking of his daughter. He hasn't seen her since she was a young girl. Of course, he went off the rails following his accident and his wife left with the daughter. She was only eight or nine. It was a tragedy, but what's to be done? I think his wife remarried." Lionel was upset for his pal.

George had woken from his slumber and surprised them with his calm contribution: "what would Fred do? I tell you what he'd do. He'd go and think it through and then he'd tackle it head on, that's what he'd do."

"You know George, you are quite right. That's exactly what he'd do and I'm going to do the same." Jane looked determined: "I'm going to talk to Rose and I'm going to do it now. You're correct Lionel, we may be in an institution, time may also be running out, but we can still do good deeds and make a difference to someone's life."

She rose from her chair, inspired, driven.

45

It was the day of the concert, as some residents would say: others referred to it as a bit of afternoon entertainment. The hall was cleared and chairs placed at one end. In the dining room, fisherman's pie or sausage and mash were being consumed, to be followed by jelly and ice cream or sponge and custard, the usual Friday fare.

Before the residents gathered, Dan carried his equipment into the hall. He set up his stool and microphone and a couple of speakers. He placed his sheet music on the floor; he stood his acoustic and electric guitars on stands. Normally, he chivvied Maisie and Betty for some pots and pans; they were usually placed on a small table for George: today, however, there was just a chair and an anonymous shape covered with a sheet. Entertainment worked well if restricted to an hour or less. In the main, residents were still sharp after dinner: any longer, the afternoon s overwhelm. Today, being almost Christmas, Dan decided to commence with some well-known seasonal songs. He would then perform a couple of modern standards, ending with a rousing Christmas carol. The hall was garlanded, the piano, not often played, was almost hidden by the large Christmas tree.

Just after half past one, Rose and her staff began ferrying in the residents. The able-bodied drifted in and sat in the rows of seats, some sat in the lounge, the double doors open. The frail and wheelchair users were placed round the outside. The staff wore elves' hats with tinsel and garlands pinned to their uniforms: the atmosphere was jolly and festive. Dan was always well received: he modified his performance to suit his audience and played for them. He never showcased his own abilities, but he sometimes included one of his own compositions, if it suited. He had several, self-penned songs which George had judged to be good: a compliment indeed.

Fred, Lionel, Spike and Jane sat at the end of the back row, Spike in his wheelchair in the aisle. They were anxious, Fred particularly. They knew of Fred's effort to grant Maurice's request, but were sceptical of a good outcome.

Dan walked in with George at his side: George, happy as ever to be performing. Dan was his hero, his kindness lifted George. The crowd clapped and cheered. George looked round for his pots and pans, worried he might not be performing. Dan led him to a chair at the side, when George sat down Dan pulled away a sheet to reveal a drum kit.

George was speechless. The drum kit was only one step up from a child's set, but George was beside himself with joy. He picked up the drum sticks and rattled off a tattoo, ending with a flourish on the cymbals. It never ceased to amaze that he, with advancing Alzheimer's, could play along with any tune: not only that, but with subtlety or vigour as required.

Dan played a few chords then straight in with 'Rocking Around the Christmas Tree,' George drummed enthusiastically. Old favourites followed, some that residents could sing along to: as ever, music and rhythm enthused even the vacant and afflicted.

Dan kept the momentum going, his easy nature and talent endeared him to all. Song followed song and in no time, the concert was halfway through. Fred was watching the door, off and on, throughout: there was no sign of the elusive entrepreneur.

"He's not going to show," Lionel said at last.

"I never thought he would: he's got no scruples that man," Spike's face mirrored his disgust: "you did your best, Fred."

The music continued, Dan completing his Christmas repertoire: George drummed in perfect time, Dan allowing him small solo slots. His hands were a blur, hitting the drums and cymbals whilst his foot beat the bass drum, he was totally absorbed. There was a small pause during which Dan whispered to Mavis: she walked briskly across the hall and reappeared with his mother, Rose.

Dan pointed to his mother: "I'd like to dedicate this song to my mum." He introduced the Paul Simon classic 'Mrs Robinson,' but altered the intro to 'Mrs Richardson' in honour of his mother. Rose smiled proudly from the side and the staff cheered. He began the lively intro, his long fingers moved over the frets with consummate ease. At that moment, Katya opened the front door to a stranger.

Nathaniel Goldman entered the hall, frowning at the assembled residents: he wondered why the hell he had come here. He wore a grey suit with white stripes and large lapels, a white fedora covered his dyed black hair. He had an embroidered pink handkerchief in a top pocket. Katya pointed to an outside seat at the front; he fumbled his way to it and sat. His sharp, narrow eyes had taken in the singer and the old demented drummer: he saw straight away that the lad was good. He noted his fair looks, good voice and good accompaniment, he was distracted though, by the sights around. He saw slumped, aging people, cripples, loonies. Jesus!

He felt a sharp prod in the back: an elderly lady with fierce eyes hissed at him. "Do you mind removing your hat." Startled, he removed his hat, apologising profusely.

A voice from behind shouted; "bighead!"

He was discomforted and looked for an escape.

Spike, sitting at the back noticed: "he's leaving, without giving that lad a chance."

Dan finished to a round of applause and cheers. Announcing the next song, he said it was a song for everyone who needed a helping hand and everyone needed that, sometimes. He announced another Paul Simon classic, 'Bridge over Troubled Waters.'

Spike turned to Jane, urgency in his voice: "Jane, you could help Dan, you could accompany him, give him a boost. You can do it: it might prevent Maurice's pal leaving."

Jane was panicked, torn between helping Dan and her concerns about her ability as a pianist. "I can't do it, I haven't played since my stroke; my hand's not the same. I'm out of practice."

Fred noticed Nat Goldman fidgeting, looking to leave. He grasped Jane's hand, looking earnestly at her: "you can do it; I know you can do it. We all know you can do it."

"It would be a wonderful gesture," Lionel asserted, "we are all with you."

Jane looked from one to another, uncertain, nervous, but she stood and made her way to the front. Her companions cheered and clapped, Spike whooping. She walked up to Dan and whispered to the bemused lad: he fiddled with his music and handed Jane some pages. Jane walked over to the piano, setting out her music and familiarising herself with her old instrument.

Meanwhile, Dan stood and announced that he was honoured to have Mrs Jane Appleby accompany him on the piano: he explained that she hadn't played for a long time and would everybody give her some support. Applause broke out and Jane flushed; a mixture of nerves and embarrassment.

At that point, Nat Goldman stood to leave: yes, the lad was good but he wasn't going to sit in an old folks' home any longer. Christ, what would his associates say? He shuffled his feet, manoeuvring to get out. A sharp pain pierced his ribs: it was the hawkish old woman again.

"Sit down, young man and don't be so damned rude, the show's nearly ended. Show some manners."

"Sorry, madam," the impresario sat down meekly and faced the front.

"Good old Miss Faversham," Spike was gleeful.

There was a pause: Dan and George watched Jane at the piano, waiting for a signal. Jane looked at the music then down at her hands. She struck a few chords, feeling her way. Her hands felt stiff especially her weak right hand. She looked across at the audience and Nat Goldman who fidgeted: she spotted Fred who gave her a 'thumbs up,' she drew up her shoulders and gave Dan a small nod of the head.

The piano introduction started falteringly but very soon Jane, growing in confidence, found her fingers loosening: her confidence grew. Her hands hovered over the keys, fingers stroking the notes. Her touch, gossamer light, produced gentle, tinkling music. The introduction was so simple, yet demanded the audience's attention: the room fell hushed, gripped by the sweetness of the music all eyes were fixed on its source.

Jane glanced up and gave an admiring Dan, an almost imperceptible nod. His clear voice rose quietly to start, merging with the bell like notes of the piano. As the song progressed, the clarity and volume rose: an emotion stirred in the hearts of the audience; the beauty of the song, with its haunting lyrics, touched nerves. Dan sang alone, of course, with no one to duet with him. The volume rose steadily to the glorious crescendo, his voice easily reaching the highest notes. The finale was so emotionally draining that tears ran down many a face. Fred, who had no ear for music, sat transfixed, mouth open. The song ended with a silent room. For a moment no one moved, then, applause erupted: Spike noticed that even Nat Goldman was clapping. Surely it was a good sign? Along the row from Nat Goldman, a rippling sound intruded, Rita's raucous voice shouted out:

"Hey, Katya, Jack's done his business: filled his pants." The aroma crept along the row.

Nat Goldman rose to his feet gasping and gagging. "Sweet Jesus, God preserve us!" He clutched his pink hankie to his mouth and made for the exit. "Dear God!"

"No blaspheming!" Rita shouted, adding: "wanker!" for good measure.

"So sorry ladies, so very sorry, I'm a bit delicate, you see." He staggered down the hall, handkerchief to mouth.

"He's leaving," there was urgency in Lionel's voice.

When the impresario reached the front door, he was halted by the security lock. Fred was on his feet; he shuffled along with his sticks as fast as he could. Mavis saw Nat Goldman at the door and moved to let him out: Spike saw this and blocked her passage.

"Hang on, Mavis, hang on," Spike hissed.

Fred reached the front door dragging his foot, breathless: he placed one of his sticks on the door handle. Nat Goldman looked round startled.

"I want a word with you."

Nat Goldman was shrewd and observant: he turned and faced the breathless, stocky figure. He noticed the sticks, the down-turned mouth, the florid face, but mostly he noticed the heavy jowls, jutting jaw and determined expression. He knew straight away that this was the no-nonsense, blunt Fred Cox, the one who had spoken to him on the phone.

Fred leaned against the wall; the pain in his chest had returned causing him to grimace. His resolve never faltered, his outstretched stick emphasised the point. He spoke one word: "Well?"

They stood facing each other, Nat Goldman knew this was not a man to be cajoled, not a man to be diverted or spun a tale. He understood there was only one approach acceptable, straight down to business.

"The lad's good, I'll grant you: there could be a future for him."

The stick never left the door handle: "Could be? What's this bloody 'could be' nonsense?

Nat Goldman ran his fingers through his thinning hair: "Look, here's my card with my personal number, I rarely give this out. If the lad rings me after Christmas, I'll have something sorted."

Fred placed his brawny right hand on the impresario's bony wrist: "look, don't piss the lad about."

Nat Goldman was surprised by the intensity of the man. He paused, looking directly into Fred's eyes: "I won't."

"And don't bloody diddle him."

"I won't." Nat Goldman held out his hand and they shook on the promise as Mavis approached.

"Please good lady, let me out of this madhouse," Nat Goldman lurched towards the open door. He turned briefly to Fred: "by the way, the pianist's pretty good," then he was gone.

Fred kissed a surprised Mavis on the cheek and leant on the wall puffing his cheeks out. Inside, 'The Twelve Days of Christmas' was rounding off the entertainment: Fred could hear the piano, everyone was joining in.

46

Christmas Eve was hectic: the staff bustled, Jane Richardson was everywhere, organising, greeting visitors, checking preparations for Christmas day. There was a magical feel to the festivities: many residents felt a child-like excitement. It was a fact that children gloried in the wonder of Christmas and parents shared in that excitement, it was also a fact that the anticipation and thrill diminished with middle-age: the magic faded when children grew up and left. With advancing years, some of that lost excitement and childish wonder returned. As grandchildren appeared it was rekindled: even without grandchildren a childlike anticipation often returned with old age.

At the dinner table, talk centred on Dan's concert the previous day. Everybody was on good form. Fred Cox was relaxed, almost jovial: he fussed over Jane Appleby; he was delighted by her musical assistance in yesterday's triumph. Praise was lavished by all and Jane was thrilled, not only with the praise, but with the fact that she had played her beloved piano once again: she now knew she could do it and would continue. George received many a pat on the back for his drumming masterpiece. He continuously shook his head, smiling to himself: the memory would be imprinted in his mind for many a while.

"I didn't think you were going to pull it off, Fred, but you did it," Lionel's pleasure was shared.

"It was touch and go," Fred mused, "but everybody played their part. Good luck to the lad, he's good."

"Goldman met his match, eh, Fred? A Tory capitalist defeated by a bigger Tory capitalist. Eh?"

"Piss off Trotsky! Get on with your free dinner."

Later, visitors came and went: some for ten minutes, some for an hour. A few sat all day with their loved ones. Most bore gifts, wrapped parcels, cards and flowers: many were unnecessary, not required. Slippers and socks were useful but, in many cases, boxes of chocolates, biscuits and more jumpers were gifts that eased consciences: a feeling that something must be presented. Most residents were happy with a greetings card and a visit; they had little need for much else.

Fred and Jane sat chatting with Lol and Mercedes: Jane was always included. Mercedes was grateful and wondrous of the changes in her father's temperament: she had never seen him so relaxed and content. This kind, refined lady seemed to have calmed the grumpy old man; he was particularly relaxed today, as if he had dealt with all his demons. Mercedes wondered what spell The Laurels had cast on her father. Whatever it was, she was grateful.

Spike, Lionel and George sat together chatting. George and Spike never had visitors: Lionel was occasionally visited by a nephew who lived in Scotland, his son, now an American resident, rarely travelled to Britain. George was unconcerned, he had no relatives: he was happy with his lot. Spike had shared a room with Lionel for a few years, they gelled together at once. Spike, initially, was withdrawn, bitter with his messed-up life. Lionel was calm, steady, intellectual: he coaxed Spike, gently drawing him out of his depression. He was patient and understanding. Soon Spike healed and his good nature surfaced. Spike doted on Lionel who was like a father to him: he would listen quietly to Spike's incessant chatting, chipping in now and again with a comment or advice. Although Lionel was fit and wiry, Spike dreaded any misfortune that might arise due to his advancing age: he would be lost without him. For Lionel, Spike was like a second son, he loved his quick wit and banter: they even shared the same political beliefs. Spike's good humour, kindness and concern for everyone endeared him to Lionel, indeed everyone. There was a hidden sadness in Spike's make-up, though, and Lionel knew it.

Cyril received a visit from the family with the complaining, mouthy mother. The same woman who Fred had once castigated. Since then, they had been more respectful of Cyril's dementia and appreciative of The Laurel's care. They engaged with him and made a greater effort: they chatted, telling him of family events, talked about the weather, even the two sullen sons spoke once or twice.

After they left, Cyril opened a present, a box of toffee. Christmas wrappings were quietly removed and soon Cyril was chomping: he was like a naughty child, gorging before anyone found out. He crammed the toffee lumps into his mouth, his cheeks bulged; his mouth was so full that he couldn't swallow. The toffee juice ran down the sides of his mouth and onto his collar.

The 'snooty couple,' as Spike called them, were visiting Albert. They were just passing when something fell on the floor at Cyril's feet. The lady, she who boasted of her holiday cruise, who Fred had also upset, bent to pick it up. She smiled condescendingly at Cyril and the others. She plucked the object off the floor and let out a squeal, a look of disgust on her face. She flapped her hands, as if ridding herself of something unspeakable. Mandy, the plump carer, hastened over, concerned.

"Cyril!" she said with mock horror, "what have you been up to? Oh no!" She picked up his discarded false teeth which were entombed in a chewed mass of toffee. She showed them, with relish, to the snooty lady who backed off out of the room. "Mmm, a bit of work needed here, Cyril, it's not Christmas day yet, you know, I think, from now on, toffee's rationed."

Spike, George and Lionel were sitting chatting. Spike had his back to the door and hadn't noticed the young woman and small child enter the room. George greeted the little girl with a big smile, the way old folks often do; delighted to see a child: "hello, hello: who are you?" The girl smiled at him shyly.

Spike turned in his wheelchair to see who it was: he sat motionless, staring at the woman. She stared back and then a smile spread over her face. She held the little girl's shoulders and moved her forward slowly: "come on Mia, let's say hello to granddad."

 Still rooted, recognition dawned on Spike. The little girl approached nervously but smiling, Spike held out his arms and she moved into his embrace. He hugged his granddaughter with one arm and his daughter with the other. For a while no-one moved then Spike pulled back, tears streaming down his cheeks: the daughter wept also.

"Don't cry, granddad, don't cry," the little girl responded, concerned.

Spike hugged her and gripped his daughter's hand tightly, laughing through his tears: "I'm not really crying, I'm just very happy to see you, very happy."

Lionel took George by the arm: "come on old pal, let's have a game of draughts. We'll leave Spike together with his family: I think he's just had the best Christmas present ever."

47

Christmas day dawned, bright and cold: there was no snow to complete a traditional scene, but a hoar frost coated grass and trees. Fred sat on his bed looking out of the window. That he took time to observe his surroundings would have surprised once, that he also found interest in nature's creatures would have seemed a fantasy.

He watched a tiny 'Jennie Wren,' as Josh called the bird, flitting restlessly beneath the window: its short, cocked tail stood vertical and the chestnut brown on its back stood out against the frost. A flock of mixed birds jostled for position on a hanging bag of peanuts across the lawn, Fred didn't know the types of bird but could see they were of mixed colours. A movement under a Laurel bush caught his eye: it was the black and white cat, the same cat that he encountered when he first arrived at The Laurels, the same cat that he treated with a scowl and hostility.

He stood and pulled something from his bedside drawer and opened the window: the cat looked up. He reached down and the cat rubbed itself against his hand taking a titbit from him.

"Now clear off and leave the birds alone." Fred sat down, breathless, the dull pain in his chest ever present. There was no Josh to visit today and no fag and coffee to enjoy. Still, it was Christmas day. He thought about Christmases he had spent alone: he'd exiled himself after his wife died; Mercedes did her best, inviting him for Christmas, all offers were refused. The only thing he would accept was a plated dinner at his flat. Now, he was glad of the company of friends at The Laurels.

He finished his ablutions and emerged from his room, heading for breakfast. He dragged his foot, leaning on his sticks. There was no real improvement in his mobility: he had refused physiotherapy and any further hospital appointments. He considered it a waste of time and effort.

After breakfast, Father Murphy and choristers gathered in the hall and sang carols: The Laurels probably enjoyed more of a traditional Christmas than any family could hope for. The atmosphere was warm and welcoming: those of the staff that were rostered for Christmas day were determined to make it enjoyable and everyone mucked in. Port and sherry tots were handed out to all who could indulge.

At dinner, the full works were laid on. Crackers were pulled, fancy hats worn, jokes read out. A few of the staff, including cooks Maisie and Betty, sat and ate with the residents. They had cooked and prepared the three-course meal but had been ordered by Rose Richardson to take their places at the tables. Rose, her son Dan, Rose's daughter and two of her college friends waited on, alongside Katya, Mavis and Katya's fiancé Tadge. There was much frivolity and good humour.

Most visiting had been done in the morning or Christmas Eve, but one or two visitors sat and dined with their loved ones: better at The Laurels than an empty home.

Tadge, big and good natured, bustled about wearing his party hat and apron: he poured drinks, fussed over residents and charmed the ladies. Rita, as ever, giggled with childish delight when he kissed her hand. She returned the compliment gleefully pinching his backside when he bent over. George clapped and drummed on the table as each course was served. Rose and the volunteer waiting staff were to eat together afterwards.

Tea trolleys laden with plated meals were carried via the lift to the nursing floor and served to the bedridden. On this floor Rev. Tom and a few volunteer parishioners sang carols and helped serve up meals. As Spike observed, Rev. Tom would turn cartwheels for a good dinner.

The volunteers and staff, along with a few relatives, fed and assisted the frail and helpless. Mary's daughter helped her mother, whilst consuming her own meal. Spike was on top form after his daughter's visit: he chatted and shouted to everyone around. Mary watched him whilst being fed. He went out of his way to communicate with the less able, he contrived questions to ask Mary and she responded with the now familiar finger signs.

When the sweet course was done and George was full of Christmas pud and custard, the lean formidable figure of 'Miss Faversham' rose from her seat and rapped the table for silence.

"Good friends, we are gathered here enjoying this sumptuous food: let us thank the Lord for our good fortune. Pause for a moment and think where we could have been in Charles Dickens' day."

She held up her hand and her audience fell hushed. She raised her face and gazed round imperiously. She began her monologue with dramatic voice and clear diction.

"It is Christmas day in the workhouse,

And the cold bare walls are bright

With garlands of green and holly..........."

The delivery was powerful and dramatic: she held the audience's attention as she once had her school pupils. The pathos of the verse touched even the most hard-hearted. She shortened the sad story to hold her audience's attention and indeed it did. She finished with a small bow of the head, there followed cheering and clapping, a release of tension from the sad dramatic ode.

"Well," Lionel lamented, "we could do with a bit of cheer after that heart-breaking rendition: I feel almost guilty."

No sooner had the words left his mouth when Rev. Tom burst through the doorway, applauding. "Bravo, bravo, madam, a wonderful rendition!" His foot skidded on a pool of gravy. He flailed the air, clutching at a low garland: he pulled it with tinsel and a sprig of mistletoe down on to his head. He tottered backwards landing in Betty's ample lap: "oh, Vicar, I didn't know you cared!" She planted a kiss on his forehead adding: "you've got odd socks on again, Vicar."

"So I have, Betty, so I have, but if it's cheered your day and you're happy, then I'm happy."

When the laughter died down, conversation took over. Gradually, people drifted into the lounge and veranda. Many, full and contented, dozed blissfully. Fred and his group sat together in the lounge, mellowed with food and drink they discussed the year's events. They recalled Christmases past: it was nostalgic but satisfying. Spike raised a glass to absent friends and they toasted Maurice and a couple of others who had departed The Laurels.

Lionel spoke with his calm and worldly manner: "we shouldn't be sad, good friends, nor should we be afraid. Old life ends, new life begins: as old friendships cease, new ones are forged. Even in this place, even in our situation, surprising things can happen to cheer us. Embrace it, good friends." He raised his glass to the company but especially to Spike.

In the evening, after tea, many residents retired to their rooms exhausted. They sat in their chairs or lay on their beds watching telly: some remained in the lounge.

Fred and Jane sat together sipping sherry. As the food, drink and good company warmed and mellowed them, a comforting lethargy crept over them.

"I think we'd better retire before we fall asleep," Jane smiled at Fred.

"You're right." It was the usual short reply from Fred but spoken softly with a fond smile.

They walked slowly into the hall and stopped, pausing at the point where Fred parted for his room. Fred leaned across and kissed Jane tenderly on the cheek: "thank you, thanks for being a good friend." Twelve months ago, Fred would have choked on those words.

Jane flushed: "I've loved every moment of it." She squeezed Fred's hand and with a glance over her shoulder walked down the corridor.

Fred watched her go: at that moment, there was no place he would rather be.

48

Christmas week was almost over and the festive spirit faded a little: too much food, drink and too many chocolates, perhaps, a general over indulgence. New Year approached bringing, for many, new hopes, new goals, a fresh start. For most at The Laurels, though, there would be no new start; it was more a matter of soldiering on. Good companions could bring cheer, fresh gossip from the staff or visitors brought interest, residents often fed off the experiences of others. Would a new year bring hope or sorrow? Here, there was time to dwell on it.

At breakfast, most people were glad of simple fare, porridge and cereals, toast and marmalade. Spike, was generally the exception tucked into the full English. "Another sausage would go down well, please, Mavis. You've got to eat well when you're on benefits: let the tax fiddlers pay for it, I say." He grinned at Fred, goading him, as usual.

Fred gave Spike the 'V' sign. He had once thought Spike a sponging scrounger, but during the time he had spent at The Laurels, he had gained respect for this good-hearted man. Self-sufficiency and thrift was a mainstay of Conservatism and Fred would never waver on that, but even he could see that without kindness and generosity of spirit, they were nothing but hard doctrines. Maybe there was some truth in Spike's assertion that Capitalist's wouldn't thrive without spenders like him: Fred smirked thinking about it.

After breakfast, Fred asked Jane if she would like a little fresh air, the morning was bright and still but very cold. Jane agreed and they wrapped up in overcoats and walked out. Their breath steamed in the crisp air. A burst of coughing caused Fred chest pain and Jane anxiety, he put his hand up to indicate he was ok and they walked slowly round the back of the house. Josh was at home with his family, but Fred proudly showed Jane the garden and 'their' shed.

"Is this where you come for those sneaky cigarettes I've heard about?"

"No, not me," Fred denied, winking. He reached up and retrieved the key, showing Jane the shed's interior. A fluttering caught their eye and Fred, rushing to impress Jane, reached round for the seed tin. He poured some seed into his hand and held it out: "keep still," he whispered.

The robin paused, head cocked on one side: no one had been to the shed for days. Fred was usually sat in his chair and who was this stranger? After a moment's hesitation, the robin flew onto Fred's hand and pecked the seed. On seeing Jane's amazed expression, Fred was proud.

Jane clasped her hands together "I'd love to do that."

"Takes a long while to build up trust," Fred shook his head doubtfully. Seeing Jane's disappointment, he said: "I'll tell you what, stretch your hand out by mine and we'll see what happens."

Jane stretched out her arm and Fred tipped a little seed into her palm. They stood, hands touching. The robin perched on the shed roof watching. After accepting Jane as harmless, the robin flew onto Fred's hand: it pecked up a few seed grains then perched on his thumb. Once again, it cocked its head on one side before flying onto Jane's outstretched palm. Jane's eyes were wide and the look of pleasure on her face produced a proud smile from Fred: he wondered why he hadn't enjoyed simple pleasures like this years ago. His life had been bound to business: now, at the end of life, he had discovered contentment in simple pleasure.

They spent some time together, the three of them. Two, world-weary, had lived out their lives, the third, waited eagerly for spring and a new beginning.

After their sojourn, they walked slowly back; the nagging pain in Fred's chest was masked by his contentment. He told Jane how Josh had introduced him to nature's delights and friend Robin. He also told her what a good bloke Josh was, a good and trusted friend. From Fred, that was praise indeed.

After dinner, Fred spotted Rose Richardson in her office, her door open: he limped in. She greeted him, looking weary. As ever, she put her best face on.

"Come on, Rose, life's not so bad."

"I suppose not, Fred, it's been a tough year though. Money's a bit tight, as ever, and now, a new boiler needed. Never mind, look on the bright side, it's always rewarding. Just wish I could offer Hannah a secure future here. By the way, thanks for what you did for Dan: I know you set it up. I feel excited about his prospects, things sound promising for him. How about you, Fred? How are you? What about hospital check-ups? What about your dickey ticker?" she chided him, shaking her head. "I was just thinking, you were such a grumpy old so and so when you first arrived: I didn't think you'd last the week. Mercedes and Lawrence didn't think you'd last a day, but here you are."

"See, I surprised you all. If you'd given me any bullshit on that first day, I'd have been gone, down that bloody drive, but you didn't." His jowled face softened into a smile: "the ticker's sound as a pound," he lied, "but I'm still that same old grumpy bugger inside."

"It's coming up to a new year: you never know; something good might crop up." Fred raised his eyebrows and nodded his head meaningfully as he left.

Jane watched him go, a thoughtful look on her face: if only.

After tea, Fred sat with Lionel, George and Spike. George was reminiscing about rhubarb.

"It was sour but we loved it. We'd chomp and suck it, faces screwed up: lovely! We'd have belly ache the next day. If you had a bit of sugar to dip in, marvellous! Best of all, if you got custard with it, lovely! Good thick, creamy custard, made with full cream milk, none of this skimmed stuff. Mind, there's nothing wrong with rhubarb and ginger jam, or even rhubarb and blackberry, better than rhubarb and apple. Mmm."

"Dear God!" Spike complained: "he has to bring jam into it every time."

"You don't dwell on the world's troubles when George is around," Lionel quipped, "except if there's a shortage of jam."

Fred spotted Jane sitting in the veranda and stood to join her. He turned to his friends: "erm, I just want to thank you lads for your good company." It was gruffly spoken and abrupt, but heartfelt.

"Hey up, what's got into Fred?" Lionel said, puzzled. They watched him walk to the veranda.

Jane had been chatting with the three elderly ladies, 'Miss Faversham' and the 'black widows', as Maurice had christened them. Fred stood to the side as they exited the veranda: he had been wary of 'Miss Faversham', he knew she had a sharp tongue, he had seen her in action.

"Good evening, Mr Cox: how are you?"

"I'm very well, thank you. I hope you ladies are keeping well." He gave them a small bow and they rewarded him with nods and smiles. He thought of Maurice's assertion that they hung upside down and drank human blood.

"Well, you've certainly charmed them, Fred."

"It's a new one for me, charm's never been one of my strong points," Fred scowled.

"You can be charming in your way," Jane smiled, "but of course, you call it bullshit."

Fred smiled at her observation: Jane understood him. They sat looking out on to the lawn; the garden was illuminated by a bright moon. They chatted for a while, comfortable in each other's company. As the evening drew on, they stood to prepare for bed; Fred gasped and held his chest. Jane was concerned and stood grasping his arms looking anxiously into his eyes: he reassured her he was fine: "Just a bit of indigestion. It serves me right: too much food."

They made their way into the hall and to their rooms to wash, or collect towels for the shower rooms. They parted, Jane kissing Fred on the cheek, still concerned.

Fred washed in his room, completed his ablutions and put on his dressing gown over his pyjamas. He sat on the bed for a while rubbing his chest and staring at the floor. He was alone: he felt lonely. He was unsettled, slightly anxious. He rose suddenly, gathered his walking sticks and walked across the hall into the corridor. He leaned on the wall, recovering his breath and watched and waited: he hoped Jane hadn't gone to bed.

He waited there for what seemed an age. At last, he saw a figure emerge from one of the shower rooms: it was Jane in her dressing gown. She spotted him as she walked back to her room, his pale face and serious demeanour worried her and she hurried to him.

"Whatever is it, Fred, do you want me to call someone?"

Fred paused, before replying, looking earnestly into her eyes: "no," he said firmly, "but I wondered..." he paused again, "I wondered... if you would come and sit with me for a while. I didn't want to be on my own."

Jane looked anxiously at him and clutched his arm. She hesitated only for a second: "of course I will, Fred, of course. Come on."

There was a look of grateful relief on Fred's face as Jane took his arm. They walked back across the hall, past the twinkling Christmas tree: Christmas was gone but it stood sentinel, awaiting the New Year.

"Would you like a small sherry, just a small tot?" Fred asked a little anxiously.

"Of course, why not, Fred." She sat on the bed watching Fred pour sherry into two mugs, tittering to herself. Fred turned, saw her laughing and laughed himself: "only the very best, you know."

They were both laughing now, tension and worry gone. Fred sat on the bed and clinked glasses: "thank you for coming."

"It's a pleasure, Fred, as long as no one thinks we are co-habiting." They giggled together like naughty children and sipped their sherries.

"Is that your aftershave I can smell, Fred?" Jane leant close, sniffing.

Fred turned, grinning. A thought entered his mind: "no, it's eau de toilette. Are you wearing the same?"

Jane looked puzzled.

Fred stuck his thumb into his incontinence pants and flipped the waistband. "You know!"

Jane looked at him for a moment then burst out laughing. She flipped her waist band: "of course, eau de toilette. What good taste we've got, Fred."

They laughed until Fred had a coughing fit and then they laughed again. At that moment nothing else mattered.

Fred woke: the first glimmer of daylight, just a hint, showed in the sky. Jane was asleep beside him, both lying on top of the bed. She lay on the wall side, adjacent to the window, her arm over Fred's chest. Fred lay on his back almost overhanging the side of the bed. He felt content; calmness enveloped him: he was at peace with the world.

A movement caught his eye, a small shadow against the hoar-frosted cherry tree. He squinted peering into the glimmering daybreak; then he heard it, that sweet song with a hint of melancholy. He could see the raised head and up-turned beak. He could see a glint in the round bright eye: he listened, charmed, a small smile on his face.

49

The truck reversed slowly and sedately: its engine ticked over, muted. The slow turning of the wheels muffled the crunch of the gravel. It gleamed in the sun, pristine: its sides announced, *'Fred Cox Transport.'*

If Fred had stood with the silent onlookers, he would have informed them that it wasn't a truck but a 6x2 tractor unit. He would have mentioned the 500 bhp turbo engine, the semi-automatic gearbox, the single reduction drive axle and more facts than they would want to know. As it was, Fred didn't stand with the crowd: his coffin rested on a wooden platform covered with green artificial grass over the truck's frame. A single wreath of red and white flowers rested on the coffin. It wasn't shaped as 'Dad' or 'Father,' but simply 'Fred.'

Two black funeral limousines stood at The Laurels' front door: the first carried Mercedes and Lawrence, the second, Rose Richardson, Jane Appleby and Katya. The occupancy of the second car had been mutually decided at The Laurels, Jane and Katya had been chosen. Most funerals of residents departed from the homes of their bereaved relatives, but for the time Fred had been resident, this was home.

Many residents stood on the drive: Lionel and George wore black ties, Spike sat in his wheelchair, respectfully holding his small tartan trilby. He was attired in a colourful shirt and jeans; his earring and tattoos were highlighted by the low January sun; staff and those that were able, stood around the coffin-bearing truck. Others looked out of the windows.

The black and white cat appeared and rubbed itself on the truck wheels, scooting off into the shrubbery when the engine started; its amber eyes watched the proceedings from cover. Lawrence thought back to when they first arrived at The Laurels and smiled. He recalled Fred pulling faces at it. The truck moved slowly forward, the two limousines following. The cortege was to drive past the truck depot where other mourners waited, then on to the crematorium.

As it processed along the drive, it passed George, Spike and Lionel. Spike doffed his trilby and Lionel bowed his head slightly. George showed the old sign of respect, gripping his collar tightly. Near The Laurels' gateway, Josh stood against an old beech tree: he was in his working clothes but this was no sign of disrespect. His face was, as always, calm and impassive. As the coffin drew level, he held his hand up in a farewell gesture.

It was all too much for the mourners in the cars: Mercedes leaned against Lol in a rare show of emotion, Lol swallowed hard, maintaining his composure. In the second car, Rose and Katya shed a tear but consoled Jane who wept openly.

Only Rose and Katya knew of Jane's presence, with Fred, on his last night. Katya had knocked and peeped round the door at 7-30. At first, she thought both were sleeping: Fred looked serene, face turned to the window, his eyes were closed and a faint smile softened his features. His pale face and still chest, however, revealed the truth. She fetched Rose, who gently roused Jane. Unaware of Fred's demise, she rose from the bed hurriedly, slightly embarrassed. It was only in Rose's office that they broke the news to her: she had been devastated. Rose and Katya comforted her and praised her humanity and concern for Fred. They vowed not to reveal Jane's presence with Fred and praised her compassion; they thought it wonderful that Fred had asked for her company in his final hours.

The cortege passed the depot where other mourners waited in their cars. A line of trucks was drawn up facing the road. As the cortege passed, a cacophony of sound assaulted their ears; the air horns of the assembled trucks rent the air with a final salute. It raised emotions and again tears flowed.

At the crematorium, there was no religious service. Fred had no great love for music but Mercedes and Lol requested a couple of 'road songs' to start and end the service. In between, the speaker gave a eulogy on Fred's life, adding that Fred was doing business to the end; those from The Laurels agreed with that. The mourners filed out, many touching the coffin in a final farewell. Outside, Lol and Mercedes greeted them. Most were business associates and employees, amongst them were Geoff Bartlett and Tadeusz of the truck recovery firm: they shook hands with Lol and kissed Mercedes.

Geoff Bartlett, pulling at his collar and looking awkward in his suit, recalled that Fred was an 'owd bugger' but a good bloke for all that; hard but fair. He asserted there'd never be another like him' he was a 'one off'. Many reminiscences were shared and there was laughter amidst the sorrow.

Mourners were invited to a community hall where refreshments were laid on. Rose, Katya and Jane made their apologies and took their leave hugging Mercedes and shaking hands and kissing Lol. Mercedes vowed that Jane would always have a friend in her and Lol: Jane was touched.

They were driven home, quiet and thoughtful: a grumpy old man had impacted on each of their lives and they had changed his. Twelve months ago, nobody would have envisaged that, least of all Fred Cox.

50

It was business as usual, at The Laurels: residents to be dressed; washed and fed, reluctant and recalcitrant charges to be coaxed and nursed. Bedpans, incontinence wear, laundry, medication, all part and parcel of a day's routine. Those whose spark still glowed amused and looked out for each other: amongst these, one or two had the energy, wit and good nature to enhance the lives of those less fortunate.

Rose Richardson pondered that very point: they had been fortunate, having a well-balanced mix in recent times. The work of herself and her team was lightened by the likes of Spike, Lionel and Jane who all showed a caring and compassionate nature. They had characters like George, Rita and indeed 'Miss Faversham' and the 'black widows': all relieved the gloom that could develop around ageing and declining residents.

Jane had taken to the piano again which was wonderful: she often sat and played. She allowed George to accompany her on his drums, if the music suited. On the advice of Lionel, Rose had asked Spike if he would help integrate and reassure new arrivals to The Laurels. It was no more than he did anyway but because Rose requested it personally Spike was proud. Rose paid him some pocket money, 'expenses', as she called it. With this, Spike provided his re-united daughter and newly discovered granddaughter with gifts and treats, as grandfathers do.

Rose sat in her office staring out of the window. She still, could hardly believe it: her daughter would soon join her at The Laurels.

When it was announced that she had been left a legacy, she couldn't take it in. There was sufficient to finance a large proportion of a new extension to The Laurels. She was shocked: not only was it totally unexpected, but Rose was worried and reluctant to accept it. She called upon Mercedes and Lol, gravely worried. She knew, in her line of business with vulnerable people, that gifts and legacies were taboo. Mercedes reassured her and told her that she and Lol were delighted with her father's gift. The money didn't affect them at all. They had the business and assets more than sufficient for their needs. They reiterated that they had never seen Fred so content whilst in her care. Rose insisted that the new extension be called 'The Fred Cox Wing', but Mercedes said no: Fred wouldn't have wanted any of that bullshit. They had laughed about it.

Rose watched Josh repairing a garden bench. He had told her of the help Fred gave his son, even though Fred never admitted it. She thought about this and recollected his solution to Katya's problems: a happy ending was certainly due there, Katya and Tadge were shortly to be married. A nice donation had been made to both Catholic and Protestant churches. Fred, a non-believer, had respected the work of Father Murphy and the Rev. Tom. The bell fund would benefit.

Other than that, Rose read out a letter to the staff and residents, it was short, a personal touch, something completely unexpected from Fred. In his own words, reflecting his own inimitable character, Fred thanked the staff, Rose and his good friends at The Laurels for making his time there pleasurable and for putting up with a miserable old bastard.

Rose left out the last phrase when she read it out to the residents but showed it to any that would take no offence.

"Good old Fred," Lionel asserted: "no pissing about!"

Lionel, Spike and George had given Fred a send-off with the usual port and sherry. Jane, Rose and Katya had sipped Jane's coffee liquor. Jane was sad and quiet, initially, but rallied with the genuine good-humoured banter of her friends. Stories abounded highlighting Fred's blunt manner, but also about his hidden qualities. They spoke of the determination he showed in sorting out the problems of others, all done in his own inimitable way. 'No fuss, no arsing about and definitely none of that shite.'

Spike concluded the eulogies, declaring, tongue in cheek: "they broke the mould when they made Fred: a Tory with a heart."

51

Birds sang around the garden, a pre-spring rehearsal. Buds were fattening and on mild, sunny days, as today, insects were emerging, ready for the frenzied activity to come.

Josh had smoked his roll-up, drank his coffee and was putting his chair away when he heard the footsteps: he looked back and saw a tall, dark-haired woman striding towards him. He recognised her as Fred's daughter, Mercedes. She had that inborn confidence and directness, typical of her father.

She smiled at him: "it's Josh, isn't it?"

He nodded, returning the smile. She reached out her hand and he shook it, nodding his head courteously.

"I know all about you, Josh, and your friendship with dad: I'd like to thank you." There was no beating about the bush; it was a familiar, to-the-point, approach.

Josh nodded; his calm face and patient manner immediately endeared him to Mercedes, as it had her father.

"I can see why Fred liked you, but I don't know how you put up with him, not many could: just you and my hubby, perhaps," she raised her eyebrows and smiled.

Josh nodded: "Fred had his moments, no doubt, but I enjoyed his company. I don't mind telling you, I've missed our little chats. We helped each other along, you know. He taught me a thing or two."

Mercedes nodded thoughtfully: "I think it worked both ways: you certainly helped him."

She placed three items on Josh's chair from a bag she was carrying. "He said you'd got to have these and you'd know what to do with them, Josh, it was his request. We're interring his ashes with Mum's, but...," she paused, "there was a proviso: I know you'll sort it. Once again, thank you from me and Lol."

She leaned across, kissed Josh on the cheek, turned and was gone.

Josh watched her walk briskly away. He picked up one of the packets: it was a pouch of loose tobacco. He put it on the top shelf in the shed.

"Fred, this is my last pack: I'll enjoy it on you but then, that's it. Healthy living you know, I've promised the family: anyway, no fun smoking alone."

The next packet was a bag of bird seed, 'Robin Mixture': smiling, he poured it into the seed tin. The last item was a jar, a small coffee jar. Josh stared at it and held it up to the light, for a moment he was puzzled. It contained a pale gritty material: it suddenly dawned on him what it was. He stood for a while deep in thought, lips pursed. His face suddenly brightened: he knew what to do.

He unscrewed the lid and poured a handful into his palm. He scattered it around the shed, in the herbaceous border and under the silver birch tree, against the wall. He threw a handful into the air and watched the fine dust disperse. As it settled, down from the tree the robin flew. It scratched around in the grit.

"Hold on, Robin, I've got some seed for you." He reached for the seed tin and broadcast some on the ground. "Not that Fred would mind; he'd be happy for you to scratch about in his ashes. We understood each other, we three. What say you, Fred?"

At the front of the house, an old man emerged from a car. He looked apprehensively at the old house in front of him. He squinted up through his spectacles: a pair of Jackdaws poked twigs down one of the large chimneys, sparrows fought over nest sites under the eaves, but he saw nothing. His mind was elsewhere. He felt something brush against his leg, it was a black and white cat. It purred: he bent and stroked it, glad of a distraction, something friendly.

"Come on, dad." The daughter took his arm, his sons stood on the doorstep, apprehensive like their father: they dreaded the front door opening and what was to follow.

The door opened: a mature woman emerged from within; her face was smiling and friendly. She shook the brothers by the hand.

"Hello, I'm Rose Richardson:" she took the old man by the arm smiling, reassuring.

"Welcome to The Laurels."

Printed in Great Britain
by Amazon